BUSTED!

"There's something I've been wanting to do all evening…"

"What?" she asked breathlessly, gazing up at him in the moonlight. He was so handsome—so tall and broad-shouldered. Her heartbeat quickened at the thought that he might kiss her.

"This," Walker said as he bent to her and kissed her.

It was a gentle exchange at first, but when she willingly surrendered, he deepened the kiss.

Roni was thrilled. She knew she was being brazen to respond so passionately to Walker, but at that moment, it didn't matter.

She just wanted to be close to him.

She needed to be close to him.

Walker took her in his embrace and crushed her against him. And it was in that moment that the sound of her father's voice shattered the silence of the night.

"What do you think you're doing?" Victor bit out, outrage sounding in his voice.

They broke nervously apart.

"Oh! P-Papa—" Roni stammered as he confronted them.

"Dr. Reynolds—" Walker didn't cower. He stood up to her father, stepping forward to confront him.

Victor turned on Walker, fury blazing in his condemning gaze. "I think you'd better leave us right now."

WANTED: The Half-Breed

Bobbi SMITH

LEISURE BOOKS NEW YORK CITY

To Quinn Everett, my fourth perfect grandson!

A LEISURE BOOK®

June 2008

Published by

Dorchester Publishing Co., Inc.
200 Madison Avenue
New York, NY 10016

ISBN 10: 0-8439-5850-2
ISBN 13: 978-0-8439-5850-8

The name "Leisure Books" and the stylized "L" with design are trademarks of Dorchester Publishing Co., Inc.

Printed in the United States of America.

10 9 8 7 6 5 4 3 2 1

Visit us on the web at www.dorchesterpub.com.

ACKNOWLEDGMENTS

I'd like to thank the real Stacy Whiting and Jim Geitgey for their support of the Midland Education Foundation's auction last fall in Midland, Texas, and the real Alan Protzel for his support of the auction for Annie's Hope, KMOX radio in St. Louis host John Carney's charity. And we can't forget the wonderful gang from the *Romantic Times* Conference who helped to raise funds for Kathryn Falk's S.O.S. charity (Save Our Soldiers)—Kimberly Lowe, Sandra Welch, Brenda Wagner and Sandy Leeds. You're all wonderful!

Thanks to Dee Stauffer and Dr. Carol Stauffer for their help with research, and to Denise Ulett, Carrie Mores and Debbie Mauer of the St. Charles County Library for their help, too!

Prologue

Two Guns, Texas

Young Wind Walker rode in silence beside his white father across the rugged Texas terrain. A sense of unease filled him as they neared his father's ranch, but he fought it down. Having lived his first ten years in the Comanche village with his mother, he knew true warriors never showed fear. He glanced over at his father, who was watching him.

"We'll be at the ranch soon," Paul Stevenson told him.

Wind Walker only nodded in response. Upon his mother's death some weeks before, he had gone on a vision quest in search of the strength and healing he needed to deal with his future. The message he'd received from the spirit had been powerful. A vision of blood had come to him, and the voice of the spirit had told him that he was to go and live with his blood father. It had warned him of the dangers he would face in the future, of betrayal and hardship, but it had also told him that there would be love and friendship in his life. As the vision had faded, a

single eagle feather borne on the wind had drifted
down to the ground beside him, and he knew it was
a sign. He'd taken the feather and the small stone it
had landed upon as his medicine, and he carried the
charms with him now in the small spirit bag he wore
for strength and safety on a leather thong around
his neck.

Paul understood his son's stoic reaction to the
news. He knew what a hard time the boy was going
through. When word of Star Cloud's death had
reached him at the ranch, he'd immediately made
plans to bring Wind Walker there to live with him
and his family.

As hard as he was trying to make things better for
Wind Walker, Paul realized it wasn't going to be easy
for any of them. His wife, Elizabeth, had known of
the boy's existence when they'd married and had tol-
erated his occasional trips to the village to see his
son, but she had not been happy with the prospect of
having Wind Walker coming to stay with them.
Only his young daughter Stacy had seemed open to
the boy's coming to the ranch. In her innocence, she
had loved the idea of having a big brother.

The thought of Stacy brought a half-smile to
Paul's face, and he urged his horse to a quicker pace.
There was no way he could make things easier for
his son, but he was going to do all he could to help
him fit in. With his mother dead, the boy belonged
with him.

Wind Walker kept pace with his father, knowing
that soon his life was going to change forever. His

father had told him of the ranch during his visits, but up until now, he had never imagined a time when he would live there. He had always thought of himself as a Comanche, but now he was going to live in the white world.

Paul reined in as he topped a low rise. He looked at his son as he stopped next to him.

"We're here," Paul told him. "This is your new home. It's the Bar S-$, but we call it the Dollar."

Wind Walker stared down at the ranch in the valley below. The two-story house and multiple outbuildings were an impressive sight, yet the idea of living in such a place was completely foreign to him.

Paul observed Wind Walker carefully. Though the boy's expression revealed nothing of what he was feeling, Paul could well imagine the turmoil within him. The inner strength he was displaying made Paul proud and even more determined to do everything he could to help his son through these difficult times. He was glad that he'd taken the time over the years to teach Walker some of the ways of the white man and how to speak English. It was certainly going to help him now.

"From now on, you'll be known as Walker Stevenson," he told him. "Are you ready?"

"I am ready, Father," Walker responded evenly, but in reality he wasn't. His father had warned him that not all white people would accept him, and he remembered the spirit's warning of what was to come. A part of him wanted to turn his horse around and race back to the life he'd always known, but he controlled the urge. Fiercely, he forced away the painful reality that that life was lost to him forever.

Walker followed his father down to the ranch.

Six-year-old Stacy Stevenson was currying her horse in the stable when she first heard one of the ranch hands call out that there were two riders coming in. She'd been anxiously awaiting her father's return and hurried to the doorway to see who it was. It didn't take her long to recognize him. Excited and more than a little nervous about what would happen next, she ran for the house to tell her mother.

"Mama!"

Elizabeth Whiting Stevenson had been hard at work in the kitchen when she heard her daughter's call. Wiping her hands on her apron, she went to the door to see what Stacy wanted.

"What is—?" She'd barely spoken when she caught sight of her husband and the boy in the distance, and she went still.

The moment she'd been dreading all these days had come. . . .

Paul was back, and he'd brought his half-breed son with him.

"Papa's here!" Stacy told her as she joined her there on the porch.

"Yes, he is," she said.

She had known about Wind Walker before she'd married Paul, but she had never imagined that she would meet the boy, let alone be forced to take him into her home.

Wind Walker had just spent the first ten years of his life living as a Comanche.

She shuddered inwardly at the thought, and wondered how he was ever going to fit in. Whatever happened, she knew it wasn't going to be easy for any of them to live together as a family.

Stacy watched as they rode in. It had been confusing and surprising to her when she'd first learned she had a big brother who was part Indian. Her parents had never mentioned him in her presence until just a few weeks ago, when her father had told her Wind Walker would be coming to the ranch to live with them.

Stacy studied her brother with open curiosity now as he drew near. His hair was long and black, he had on only a loincloth, leggings and moccasins, and he wore a small pouch on a leather thong around his neck. He looked every bit a Comanche, and though her father had told her there would be nothing to fear from the boy, she edged a little closer to her mother.

Paul drew rein in front of the house and dismounted, as did Walker.

"We're here, Elizabeth," Paul said, glad to finally be home. He could tell by his wife's serious expression that she was worried, and he planned to do all he could to make her comfortable with his decision to raise his son on the Dollar. He went up on the porch and kissed her gently.

Walker stayed back by the horses. He was aware that his father's wife was watching him carefully, as was the young, blond-haired boy standing at her side. His father had told him that he had a daughter named Stacy, but Walker had no idea who this boy could be. He saw no hint of welcome in their gazes, so he remained standing where he was.

"How's my girl?" Paul opened his arms to Stacy and she darted straight into his embrace.

"Fine, Papa," she told him, hugging him fiercely.

Walker was startled by the revelation that the child was not a boy, but his father's daughter. Dressed as she was in pants, a shirt and boots, Stacy looked like no girl he'd ever seen before.

Paul knew the time had come. He turned to look at Walker. "Walker, this is your stepmother, Elizabeth—"

"Hello." His greeting was awkward.

"Welcome to the Dollar, Walker." She tried to sound sincere as she managed a small, not-quite-convincing smile. It wasn't easy.

Walker made no move to join them.

"And this is your sister, Stacy," Paul finished.

Stacy looked up at her father and asked with childish earnestness, "Is he really my brother?"

"Yes, he is."

At that, she broke into a very real smile and left the porch to go to him. Remembering all the stories Stacy had heard about the Comanche, she had to admit she was a little afraid of him, but she wasn't going to let that stop her. She'd always wanted a big brother. She halted right in front of Walker and beamed up at him. "Come on. Let's go inside."

Walker was unsure of what to do.

"Come on, Walker," she insisted, not about to be put off. She took his hand and tugged him along with her. "You're home."

Glancing down at Stacy and seeing the purity of her innocence and the openness of her welcome, he allowed himself to be drawn into the house.

It was the beginning of his new life.

One Month Later

Walker was glad when Miss Lowe, the school-marm, finally dismissed class. Being in the small schoolhouse all day was testing his self-control, but Walker understood it was important that he learn how to read and write. He was slowly getting used to dressing like a white man and having his hair cut short, but he knew it would take much longer for him to adjust to being around the white children, especially since most of them made it a point to let him know he was not welcome. Walker left the building alone and headed over to where the horses were tied to wait for Stacy so they could ride out to the ranch. He still hadn't come to think of it as riding home yet.

Eight-year-old Veronica Reynolds was delighted that school was out, and she was just starting her walk home when she heard a dog's tortured howl coming from somewhere behind the schoolhouse. As the daughter of the town's only doctor, she knew the sound of pain when she heard it, and she immediately ran around to the back of the building to see what was wrong.

Roni was horrified by what she found. Lee Martin,

one of the bullies from the class, had just hit Jim Geitgey, the son of the town's banker, and knocked him down. Jim's dog must have gone after the bigger boy, wanting to defend Jim, but Lee was kicking it savagely. The dog yelped and crawled away, struggling to hide in some low-growing bushes nearby.

"Don't hurt Tiger!" Jim yelled, wiping blood from his mouth as he tried to get up. He was the smartest boy in school, but small in stature. He was no match for the stronger, meaner boy. Roni knew why Lee was after Jim today. He'd refused to let the bully copy his answers during the test that had been given that afternoon and she figured Lee had probably flunked.

"Why?" Lee sneered. "I'm having fun!" It looked like he'd broken the dog's right leg.

"Lee! What are you doing? Stop it!" Roni shouted as she ran toward them to try to help. Jim didn't seem too badly hurt, but Tiger looked as if he might be seriously injured.

"Get out of here, Roni!" Lee turned on her.

Roni refused to be intimidated by the likes of him. She kept going, determined to help Tiger. Jim's dog always waited faithfully for him outside of school, and it didn't surprise her to find that he had tried to defend his master from Lee's attack. She knew how mean Lee could be.

Lee looked furious when she didn't leave. He grabbed her by the arm just as she'd almost reached the mutt. "That dog doesn't need any help."

"Yes, he does!" she insisted.

"Let her go!" Jim demanded, getting to his feet.

Walker had been getting ready to mount up when he heard a girl shout and wondered what was going on behind the schoolhouse. Stacy had just joined him, so together they went to see what had happened. They'd just come around the corner of the building when Lee grabbed Roni. Walker watched her struggle for only a moment before speaking up.

"You heard him. Let her go," Walker ordered as he watched Roni put up a good fight. He found himself impressed by her daring.

Lee looked surprised to see Walker and Stacy standing there. Roni was still trying to get away from him, but it was obvious he wasn't about to let her go. He glared at Walker with a look of hatred.

"You think you can make me since you're such a brave warrior?" he taunted in a nasty tone.

"That's right." Walker faced off with him, ready for whatever might come next.

"This is my fight, Walker," Jim spoke up, coming to stand at his side.

"Walker, don't do anything! Wait—I'll get Miss Lowe!" Stacy called, looking amazed by the change in her brother. Walker knew she had never seen him like this before.

Lee didn't seem to care if Stacy went for the teacher. He was completely focused on finishing what he'd started with Jim and his mutt.

"Here," he laughed. "You want her? She's all yours." He shoved Roni toward the two boys as hard as possible.

Roni was caught by surprise at her sudden release.

She fell heavily to the ground as Lee turned to kick the dog again.

It was then that Walker made his move.

With perfect accuracy, he drew the hunting knife he kept hidden on him and threw it.

The deadly-looking blade pierced the ground right in Lee's path and stopped him cold.

"If you want a fight, pick on someone your own size," he challenged.

"Why you—!" Lee quickly grabbed up the knife and turned on him, weapon in hand.

"What is the meaning of this?" Miss Lowe asked. She looked horrified by the sight of Lee holding the knife so threateningly as she came hurrying around to the back of the school with Stacy.

"It wasn't my fault, ma'am. I was just defending myself!" Lee quickly told her. Accomplished liar that he was, he quickly wove a tale that she'd believe. "Jim and me were just horsing around, and then the half-breed, here, just showed up and threw his knife at me!" He handed the knife over to her.

The schoolmarm took the weapon from him. She paid no attention to Jim as she glared at Walker, her shock and disapproval over his actions obvious in the look on her face. She had made it clear that she didn't want the half-breed boy enrolled in her school for just this reason.

"You're nothing but a dangerous animal," she said to Walker. "I know now that I can't allow you to stay in school with the other children. Tell your father that you are no longer to attend classes here."

"Lee's lying, Miss Lowe! That's not what happened!" Stacy put in, defending her brother. "Tell her, Jim—Tell her, Roni—"

"Miss Lowe, it's not like Lee said—" Jim began.

"Miss Lowe," Roni quickly added. "Walker was trying to help me."

The schoolmarm silenced them both with her sternest, most censorious look. "Walker used his knife as a weapon. He could have killed someone," she said.

"This is your knife, isn't it?" Miss Lowe demanded of Walker.

"Yes," Walker answered.

"Leave the school grounds and do not come back."

She turned and walked away, keeping the weapon as proof of what he'd done.

Lee was smirking as he moved off. He'd certainly come out the victor in their confrontation.

Roni, Jim and Stacy looked shocked by the schoolmarm's decision, but Walker wasn't.

"Walker," Stacy spoke up. "What are we going to do?"

He looked down at his little sister. "Right now, we're going to take care of the dog."

They all quickly gathered round as Jim and Roni carefully pulled Tiger from where he was hiding in the brush, cowering in pain.

"How is he?" Jim asked Roni.

"He looks bad," Roni answered, examining Tiger as best she could. "His leg is broken and I think maybe some of his ribs. We'd better take him over to my father. He'll be able to help him."

Jim carefully lifted his injured dog into his arms and stood up.

Roni looked up at Walker as she and Jim started toward her father's office.

"Walker—"

Walker was standing with Stacy at his side, watching them, and he met Roni's gaze across the distance.

"Thank you," Roni told him. "There's no telling what Lee might have done if you hadn't shown up when you did."

"Yeah, Walker," Jim said. "Thanks for your help. I'm just sorry Miss Lowe didn't believe us."

"So am I," he said tersely, unsure what he would face when he returned to the ranch and told his father of the teacher's orders.

He and Stacy turned away to go back to their horses and make the ride out to the Dollar.

It was much later that night when Paul returned from his trip to town to speak to the schoolmarm. He wasn't in the best of moods as he entered the house to find Walker and Stacy still waiting up for him.

"Why aren't you in bed?" he demanded.

"I let them stay up," Elizabeth defended them.

"What did Miss Lowe say, Father?" Walker asked as he came to stand before Paul.

Paul pulled Walker's knife out of his belt where he'd been carrying it. He handed it back to his son. "I tried to convince her to let you return to the classroom, but her mind's made up."

Walker was not surprised by her decision as he stared down at the knife he held in his hand. "I see."

"What are we going to do?" Elizabeth asked in a

worried tone. "Walker's been having a hard enough time trying to fit in, and now this—"

"Well, I think I've got that worked out already. Dan Geitgey stopped me while I was in town, and he told me how much he appreciated the way you helped Jim out today."

"He did, Papa. Walker was real brave, standing up to Lee that way," Stacy put in.

"So I understand." Paul's stern mood eased and he smiled down at his daughter. He looked at Walker. "It seems you've made yourself a good friend in Jim, and, fine student that he is, he's volunteered to tutor you here after school."

"Jim is real smart," Stacy told Walker earnestly, sounding much happier now that things were going to turn out all right. "He'll teach you good—maybe even better than Miss Lowe!"

Walker nodded, almost relieved that he didn't have to return to the schoolhouse. "I do have one question, Father."

"Yes, Walker?"

"How is the dog?"

"According to Dan, Dr. Reynolds bandaged Tiger up and he should be all right."

Finally, Walker smiled.

Chapter One

*R*oni stood before the full-length mirror in her bedroom, critically studying her own reflection. She had arranged her dark hair up in a sophisticated style, and she was wearing the new blue gown her mother had made for just this occasion. The bodice was modestly cut, and the fitted waistline enhanced her slender figure. It wasn't often she got to dress up this way, and she was excited. Social events like the dance were rare in Two Guns, and she could hardly wait for the social to begin. She was going to get to see Walker again.

Roni's heartbeat quickened at the thought of him. They had had a secret rendezvous out by the creek near the Dollar the week before, and the memory of their stolen kisses still had the power to thrill her. She was eagerly looking forward to being in his arms, dancing with him tonight. She knew her parents didn't really approve of Walker, but she didn't care. She just wanted to be with him.

Satisfied that she looked her best, Roni had just turned away from the mirror when her mother walked into the room to check on her.

"Are you about ready?" Helen Reynolds asked, smiling at the sight of her daughter looking so ladylike.

"Well, I think so. What do you think?" Roni asked as she faced her mother.

"I think you look absolutely beautiful," she told her. "My little girl has grown into a lovely young woman."

"Really?"

"Really," she assured her. "Now, let's get downstairs. Your father's ready to go, and you know how much he dislikes being kept waiting."

"But we're worth the wait, don't you think?"

"Yes, we are," her mother agreed.

They were both laughing as they left Roni's bedroom. They started down the steps just as her father came out of the parlor.

Victor Reynolds smiled at their laughter. "You two sound like you're already having fun."

"We are." Roni went to kiss him on the cheek.

"I am one lucky man," he said, offering each an arm as he escorted them from the house. "I'm showing up at the dance with the two best-looking ladies in town."

"Victor, you are such a charmer," Helen told him. "I just hope there are no medical emergencies tonight. I don't want you to get called away."

They were all smiling as they made their way to the town hall where the dance was being held.

* * *

"What is he doing here?" elderly town gossip Matilda Wentworth muttered to her friend, Amanda Rawlings, when she spotted Walker Stevenson arriving at the dance.

"I don't know, but keep your voice down. This is supposed to be a fun evening," Amanda censored her.

"Well, it would be more fun if that—that half-breed wasn't here," Matilda hissed. "What was Paul thinking when he brought him to live on the Dollar?"

Amanda glanced over at her companion. Matilda was known for being opinionated, and over the years she'd made no secret of the fact that she had no use for the Stevenson boy. "He's Paul's son, and he's grown into a fine young man, considering—"

"Exactly—'considering.' Considering he spent ten years living like an animal in the Comanche village!" Matilda pointed out haughtily.

Amanda fell silent. She knew there was no use in trying to change her friend's mind about this.

Matilda went on. "The rest of the folks around here just go along with including him because Paul's so rich. I'll just bet if his father didn't have the best ranch in the area, there wouldn't be so many people eager to put up with the bastard." Matilda had always made a point of knowing everyone else's business in town, and she had become very good at it over the years.

"Matilda!" Amanda was truly shocked by her language. "Hush! Dr. Reynolds is coming with his wife and daughter!"

* * *

"Why, Roni, you look nice tonight." Matilda Wentworth said, eying Roni with critical interest.

"Thank you, Mrs. Wentworth," Roni replied respectfully. She knew that was high praise coming from the older woman, who rarely had a kind word to say about anyone.

"Good evening, ladies." Helen joined them.

"Are you ready to have a wonderful evening?" Matilda asked.

"Oh, yes," Roni answered looking around excitedly to see one of her girlfriends across the room. "Mother, there's Sherry—"

"Run along and have fun, dear."

Victor and Helen moved away from the gossipy old ladies and set about enjoying themselves, too.

Roni was on her way to visit with her friend, but she never made it. Ted Lawson, one of the rowdier hands from a neighboring ranch, cornered her and wasted no time getting her out onto the dance floor.

Walker was standing off to the side of the room with Jim when he saw Roni arrive with her parents. She looked so stunning, he couldn't take his eyes off her. He thought about the time they'd shared up by the creek and knew he had to dance with her as soon as he could.

"What are you looking at?" Jim noticed how Walker had gone quiet all of a sudden.

"Roni."

Jim glanced in the direction Walker was looking

just as Ted started dancing with Roni. "Now I understand your reaction," he chuckled. "She is one fine-looking woman. Too bad Ted got to her first. He's a lucky man."

"He's lucky, all right" Walker agreed, "but I'm not so sure about Roni."

They both watched and grew a little concerned for her safety as Ted bounced rambunctiously about the floor with her.

"You thinking about cutting in?" Jim asked. "If you don't, I will. I'd hate to see her end up at her father's office tonight getting patched up because of Ted."

"You're right. I'd better get her away from him."

Walker made his way through the maze of dancers. Ted was moving wildly about the room, so it wasn't easy to catch up with them, but Walker finally managed to cut in. Ted wasn't happy about the interruption, but Walker didn't care. He just wanted Roni.

"Mind if I finish up this dance?" Walker asked Roni.

"Thank you," she told him in a low voice, grateful for his bold move as she went into his arms. "I don't know how much longer I could have lasted with Ted."

"Glad to help."

Roni followed his lead in the spirited dance and found herself caught up in the moment.

"I never knew you were such a good dancer," Roni said, smiling up at him.

"I'm not," he told her with a wry smile. "Ted just makes me look good."

She laughed at his quip, and then they both fell silent to enjoy these moments together.

When the music stopped a short time later, they moved almost reluctantly apart.

"If you need rescuing again, just let me know," he said.

"You do have a way of showing up when I need help the most," she told him.

At the side of the dance floor, Helen Reynolds noticed that Matilda Wentworth was watching Roni intently, her expression one of complete disapproval. She wondered what was putting such a sour look on the old gossip's face.

"What was Roni thinking dancing with the likes of him?" Helen heard Matilda ask Amanda.

"Roni is not your daughter, so it doesn't matter what—"

"What doesn't matter?" Helen asked, joining the ladies.

Amanda cast Matilda a warning look, but it didn't stop her from putting her two cents' worth in.

"Did you see who cut in on your daughter while she was dancing with Ted Lawson?"

"Actually, no, I didn't." Helen looked out across the dance floor, but saw only Roni talking with her girlfriends across the room.

"It was that—that half-breed—" Matilda informed her.

"I see. If you ladies will excuse me." Helen moved stiffly away from them, knowing once Matilda got started there was no stopping her.

As she left she saw Matilda shoot Amanda a smug, superior look and then turn her attention back to watching the dancers.

Helen sought out her husband and took him aside to speak with him. She told him what she'd learned about Walker and Roni.

"It was only one dance," he tried to reassure his wife.

"I know you're right, but it's not like they're children anymore," she countered, worried.

"I'll keep an eye on things," he promised.

Roni enjoyed herself as the night went on. She danced with Walker again and with Jim and several of the other young men, but even as she danced with the others, the memory of how wonderful it had felt to be in Walker's arms stayed with her. When the time for the Ladies' Choice dance drew near, she knew what she was going to do. She found Walker in the back of the room, standing near the refreshment table with Jim and several of the ranch hands from the Dollar.

"It's almost time for the Ladies' Choice," Roni told him. "Are you ready?"

"If he's not, I am," Jim put in, sounding more than willing to accommodate her.

"She's mine," Walker declared. He stepped up and took her by the hand just as the dance was announced. He wasn't about to let the chance to dance with Roni again pass him by.

Victor had known that the Ladies' Choice was coming up, and he'd deliberately gone looking for his daughter. He'd been keeping an eye on her for most of the evening and had grown troubled when he'd seen her dance with Walker a second time. Victor had just about reached her when he heard Walker claim her as his own and lead her out onto the floor.

The thought of the half-breed even having such thoughts about his daughter disturbed Victor. True, Walker was the son of a rich rancher, and he had managed to adapt to living a civilized life, but there could never be any denying he was part Comanche. It took all of Victor's self-control not to make a scene. He stood back, silently wondering what to do about his daughter's errant behavior. He thought they had raised her right. She should have known better than to dance with Walker so many times and risk ruining her reputation.

"Are you having a good time tonight?" Walker asked Roni.

"As long as I'm dancing with you," she said, thrilled to be in his arms again.

He smiled at her compliment. "You know, we could go outside for a while—"

"Let's," Roni agreed breathlessly.

Walker skillfully maneuvered them near the side

door and quickly led her from the building, holding her hand.

They moved away from the hall off into the shadows of the night, stopping in a quiet space near a small grove of trees.

Walker looked around and once he'd made certain they were really alone, he told her, "There's something I've been wanting to do all evening . . ."

"What?" she asked breathlessly, gazing up at him in the moonlight. He was so handsome—so tall and broad-shouldered. Her heartbeat quickened at the thought that he might kiss her.

"This," Walker said as he bent to her and kissed her.

It was a gentle exchange at first, but when she willingly surrendered, he deepened the kiss.

Roni was thrilled. She knew she was being brazen to respond so passionately to Walker, but at that moment, it didn't matter.

She just wanted to be close to him.

She needed to be close to him.

Walker took her in his embrace and crushed her against him. And it was in that moment that the sound of her father's voice shattered the silence of the night.

"What do you think you're doing?" Victor bit out, outrage sounding in his voice.

They broke nervously apart.

"Oh! P-Papa—" Roni stammered as he confronted them.

"Dr. Reynolds—" Walker didn't cower. He stood up to her father, stepping forward to confront him.

Victor turned on Walker, fury blazing in his condemning gaze. "I think you'd better leave us right now."

He kept his voice low as if he didn't want anyone else to hear them and learn of Roni's scandalous behavior, but there was no mistaking the seriousness of his intent.

It was plain that Walker didn't want to desert Roni. He looked down to where she was standing by his side. "Roni?"

"Go on," she said.

"Are you sure?"

She nodded, miserably.

"You heard me, boy," Victor replied threateningly.

Walker said nothing as he moved off into the night, leaving father and daughter alone.

"We're going home, right now, young lady."

"But, Papa—" she started to protest.

The look he gave Roni silenced her, and, unnerved, she said nothing more. Her father had never been this angry with her before, and she wasn't sure what was to come.

"Wait right here while I get your mother." It was an order.

Roni did as she was told.

Much later that night, Roni sat alone in her bedroom, staring out the window, unable to sleep. The trip home had been made in complete and total disapproving silence, and she had been sent directly to her room once they'd reached the house. She longed to see Walker again, to tell him none of this was his fault, but she knew that wasn't going to happen—not any time soon. Not from the way her parents were acting.

Sighing, Roni stretched out on her bed and sought sleep, unsure of what the morning would bring. Sleep proved elusive, though, as exciting memories of Walker's kiss and being in his arms lingered in her mind.

Victor and Helen sat closeted in the study, weighing the results of the decision they'd just made about their daughter's future.

"I think she'll be very happy," Victor said, trying to convince himself as well as his wife that they were right.

"Do you really?" Helen asked worriedly.

"Roni's always shown great interest in wanting to become a doctor, and she can accomplish that by going back east to school to complete her studies," he reassured her.

"But she'll be so alone—"

"You can travel with her and stay with family there until it's confirmed that she's been admitted to the medical school. It's not going to be easy for her. The prejudice against women doctors is very real, but I believe she's strong enough and smart enough to deal with it."

"I hope you're right, but what about you? You'll be here all by yourself until I can get things worked out for Roni."

His expression was fierce as he told her, "I'll miss you both. Have no doubt about that, but it'll be worth it to get her away from Walker's influence."

They shared a troubled look, worrying about the results of the decision they'd just made concerning their beloved only daughter's future.

"We'll tell her first thing in the morning," Helen agreed.

Two Weeks Later

Walker rode to the top of the low rise and reined in. He had a clear view of the road leading out of Two Guns and knew he would be able to see the stagecoach when it left.

He hadn't had the chance to be with Roni since the night of the dance. He'd gone to her house to speak with her the day after, to find out how things had gone with her parents, but her mother had told him Roni wasn't home and not to come back. He'd only found out last night from Jim that Roni was leaving this morning to go back east and study to become a doctor like her father.

Walker had wanted to see her before she left, but had realized that it wasn't going to happen. Her father had made it perfectly clear the night of the dance that he didn't want her anywhere near him.

In the distance, now, he saw the stage coming. He watched in silence as it passed by, traveling east. He thought about trying to catch up with the stage to tell Roni good-bye, but she hadn't responded to the note he'd sent her several days before, so he stayed where he was.

The stage moved on out of sight.

Walker headed back to the Dollar.

Chapter Two

Five Years Later

The annual festival had been going on all day and was a big success. It seemed just about the whole town and most of the ranchers from the outlying areas had turned out for the final event tonight: the dance. The hall was crowded, and everyone seemed to be having fun.

Off to the side of the dance floor, Matilda was keeping careful watch over the evening's activities.

"You know, Amanda," the elderly gossip began, "Roni Reynolds is back in town."

"Yes, I heard that, and I'm looking forward to seeing her again. We're so blessed that she decided to come back to Two Guns and take over her father's practice. We need a good doctor in town."

Matilda gave a derisive snort. "I doubt it was medical opportunity that called her back here."

"What are you talking about?"

"I'm talking about the half-breed. Don't you remember all the talk about her and Walker before she went back east to school? Well, it'll be interesting tonight, to see if they pick up where they left off."

Amanda couldn't believe Matilda remembered all the details from so many years ago.

"You'll just have to keep watch," she told her friend, not wanting to start an argument.

"Don't worry," Matilda said with a confident grin. "I will."

Walker was standing with Jim, Chet Harrison and Stacy at the side of the dance floor.

"You've got yourself one lovely woman," Jim complimented Chet on his recently announced engagement to Stacy. When he had first heard the news, he'd been troubled. He cared for Stacy. He always had, but quiet man that he was, he'd never let her know the truth of his feelings for her. He deeply regretted that omission now for she'd accepted Chet's proposal, and they were to be married the following spring.

"Yes, I do," Chet agreed, smiling down at Stacy as he slipped an arm around her waist and drew her closer to his side.

Jim knew he had bought a ranch in the area some four years before and had been working it hard all this time. He'd noticed Stacy the year before and had started wooing her right away. The folks around Two Guns agreed she had it all—good looks with her blonde hair and shapely figure, and money, since the Stevenson ranch, the Dollar, was the most successful ranch in the area. She would be the perfect wife.

Stacy smiled up at her fiancé, all the love she felt for him shining in her eyes. "And I've got myself one good man."

"Well, look who's finally shown up—the new doc, herself," Jim said to the others as he caught sight of Roni making her way toward them.

Walker had not seen Roni since she'd returned from back east several weeks before. He glanced in her direction now and found he couldn't look away as she paused to greet some of the other townsfolk. The pale green, modestly cut gown she was wearing fit her perfectly, and she had styled her hair down around her shoulders in a tumble of soft dark curls. Roni had always been a pretty girl, and she had grown into a striking young woman.

"It's about time you got here," Jim teased Roni when she finally joined them. "I was wondering where you were."

"There was a last-minute emergency with one of the Nelson twins," she explained.

"Anything serious?" Stacy asked.

"No. Just a little too much roughhousing. Their mother thought one of the boys had broken his wrist, but it was only sprained. I bandaged him all up and he should be fine."

"Well, that's good news," Jim added.

Roni smiled up at him, and then she turned to Walker. "Walker. It's good to see you."

Roni had recognized Walker the moment she'd spotted him from across the room, standing there with Jim, who was now the town's banker. They were two of the tallest men in the room, and they were definitely two of the handsomest.

"You, too," Walker returned, his dark-eyed gaze warm upon her.

"You look lovely tonight—not that that's unusual for you," Jim told her.

"Jim, you are such a charmer," Roni laughed. She was excited about the evening to come. This was the first chance she'd had to see everyone again and renew her friendships.

Stacy spoke up quickly, "Roni, I want you to meet Chet—my fiancé."

"Your fiancé? Congratulations, Stacy!" Roni looked at the handsome man standing beside Stacy and smiled. "It's nice to meet you."

"Thanks. It's nice to meet you, too. I've heard a lot about you."

Roni laughed. "Good things, I hope."

"Of course," he told her with a grin.

"When did you come to Two Guns?" she asked.

"Chet bought the old Jones place a few years ago," Stacy told her.

"So, you've been turning the ranch around, have you?" Roni remembered how rundown it had been.

"I'm working on it," Chet answered confidently. "Stacy was telling me there had been some talk going around for a while that you were thinking about staying back east and setting up your practice there." Stacy had told him that Roni's mother had passed away several years before, and that her father had died of a fever the previous summer.

"I thought about it, but even with my parents both gone now, this is still home. I'm glad to be back."

"Think you're going to have any trouble convincing people you're a good doctor?" Jim asked, joining in the conversation. "Most folks think being a doctor is a job meant only for men."

"I know. My father warned me about that, and I heard a lot of talk about the prejudice in the East. I'm hoping here in Two Guns everybody will know that I'm my father's daughter and judge me accordingly."

They all knew everyone in the area had highly respected and trusted Dr. Reynolds.

The musicians started up a new tune, and Chet wasted no time getting Stacy out on the dance floor. Before Walker could ask Roni to dance, Jim claimed her.

"I've been waiting all week just to dance with you," Jim told Roni as he took her arm and led her out among the other couples.

"I can still cut in," Walker said, grinning easily and planning to do just that.

He waited until about halfway through the dance and then made his move, deftly cutting in on his friend.

They were all laughing as Jim reluctantly turned Roni over to him.

When Roni went into Walker's arms, she was surprised by the shiver of sensual awareness that trembled through her at being so close to him. They began to move together in rhythm with the music.

As Walker squired her around the dance floor, Roni looked up at him, studying the strong line of his jaw and his lean, handsome features. He sensed her gaze upon him and glanced down, and their gazes met. For a moment, they were lost, and then they both smiled.

"I remember another time when we danced like this. You'd just saved me from being trampled by Ted."

"Well, you don't have to worry about Ted anymore. His whole family moved on a year or so ago."

"You mean it's safe to be out on the dance floor in Two Guns now?"

"That's right."

They laughed and then both fell silent as other memories from that night returned. They enjoyed their time together, but as soon as the music ended, Jim was there to dance with her again.

As the evening progressed Roni visited with friends and had a good time dancing with a number of the bachelors in town. As nice as her other dancing partners were, though, she found herself occasionally scanning the crowd, looking for Walker. When he finally sought her out and asked her for the next dance, she was delighted.

Again, they moved together about the floor in perfect rhythm.

"I've been dancing so much tonight, we haven't had much time to talk yet," she said.

Walker grinned down at her. "Do you want to go outside for a while?"

Roni still remembered the last time they'd done that, and she didn't hesitate to answer, "Yes."

Walker expertly danced her over toward the side door. They slipped outside into the welcoming darkness and made their way to a quiet place, not too far from the building to talk.

"I'm glad you're back," Walker said, gazing down at her and finding her even more beautiful in the moonlight.

"So am I," she admitted. She fell silent for a moment, just enjoying the peace of the evening, and then asked him, "How have you been? I've thought about you over the years. I always wondered why I never heard from you again after the dance that night."

He frowned slightly. "Didn't your parents tell you that I came to the house to see you?"

She was surprised by his words. "No. You did?"

He nodded. "The day after, I stopped by, but your mother told me you weren't home and not to come back."

"I didn't know. They never said a word. I wanted to see you again, to tell you that I was going back east to school, but it all happened so fast."

"Yes, it did." He didn't tell her how he'd watched her leave on the stage that day. "Are you glad you became a doctor?"

She told him earnestly, "Most of the time, yes. It's wonderful to know you can help someone who's in pain, that you can make things better for them. And when you bring a baby into the world, it's amazing. There are the hard times, though. When someone is so sick all you can do is try your best and hope that you've made a difference in some way. What about you? I take it you never got married?"

"No, I never married. After Father and my stepmother died, I took over running the Dollar."

"From what I hear, the ranch is still doing great. Jim told me it's as successful as ever—maybe even more so," Roni praised him.

"Thanks. Stacy helps me work it, and between the two of us, we've kept things going."

"What do you think about Stacy's engagement to Chet? She seems really happy."

"I think she is. Chet seems like a good man. What are your plans? Are you going to be happy practicing here in Two Guns?"

"Oh, yes. This is where I want to be."

Walker looked down at her, his gaze soft upon her. "I'm glad."

The look in his eyes left Roni breathless. "So am I."

The moment was magical. There alone in the moonlight, he couldn't resist the temptation to finish the kiss they had started all those years ago.

Roni didn't move as he bent to her and claimed her lips. She gave a small throaty sigh and went into his embrace. Her willingness encouraged him. Walker deepened the exchange, hungry to taste of her sweetness. It was an awakening for them both, a moment of startling passion that thrilled them with its intensity. They clung together, seared by the fire that had sparked between them, until the realization of just where they were returned, and they broke apart.

"We'd better get back inside," Roni said reluctantly.

"I know." As tempted as Walker was to take her back in his arms, he controlled the need to hold her again.

They had almost reached the doorway when Jim appeared in the entrance, looking for them.

"There you are! Come on, Roni! It's time for us to have another dance!"

"No, you're going to have to wait, Jim," Walker told him. "I've already claimed Roni for this one."

She offered no protest as Walker guided her out to join the other couples on the dance floor, leaving Jim to look on.

Everyone in Two Guns knew rancher Ben Thompson was a mean man, and when he got drunk, he got even meaner. Big and stocky, and fast on the draw, he would take on just about anybody in town when he got drunk enough. When he'd started drinking earlier in the evening at the Ace High Saloon, the other men in the bar took care to stay as far away from him as they could to avoid trouble. The relief was great when Ben and his ranch hands finally left the bar. The men heard him declare he was heading over to the dance, and they couldn't help wondering what kind of trouble he was going to stir up over there.

Ben and his boys were feeling real good as they entered the hall. They stopped just inside the door to look around, and Ben spotted Walker Stevenson dancing with Roni Reynolds. He'd heard the talk around town of how she'd come back to take over her father's medical practice, and it infuriated him that the half-breed thought he was good enough to be socializing with the folks in town, let alone dancing with the new doc. Fury ate at Ben, and he smiled coldly as he tried to figure out the best way to get at Walker.

Ben hated the Stevenson family with a passion. Their ranches adjoined one another, and through the years old man Stevenson had made the Dollar the most successful ranch in the area. It hadn't mattered to Ben that Paul Stevenson had been an honest man with a fine reputation. To Ben, his success had been infuriating.

Ben knew he'd been lucky over the years that Paul hadn't caught him rustling Dollar cattle. Then when Paul died and left the ranch to his half-breed bastard son and Stacy, Ben had been even more outraged. The fact that the half-breed was running the Dollar now, and it was as successful as ever, made Ben hate them that much more.

"Well, boys, look what we got here," he muttered to the hands standing nearby. "If it ain't our good friends from the Dollar."

Mick Jones knew exactly what his boss was thinking, and it worried him. There were a lot of innocent people at the dance, and he didn't want to see anybody get hurt. "Boss, this ain't the time to go startin' anything—"

"Shut up," Ben ordered harshly. "I'm going to

have me some fun tonight after all." He looked over at his men, challenging them. "I pay your salaries. Are you with me?"

They nodded, knowing they had no choice if they wanted to keep their jobs. They hung back and waited to see what their drunken boss was going to do.

Stacy was having a wonderful time dancing with Chet. This was the first social event they'd attended since they'd become engaged, and she was enjoying every minute of it—especially getting to dance with him and be in his arms.

"You know what we could do tonight, don't you?" Chet was smiling down at her, his gaze hungry upon her.

"No, what?" Stacy was puzzled by his question.

"We could sneak out of here and run off to the justice of the peace—"

"You are so romantic." She was delighted by his daring suggestion, but she had already started planning the wedding, and she wanted to be married in church.

"Then let's do it," he urged, wanting to make her his own as quickly as possible. "Next year is too long to wait."

"You know I'm tempted, but—"

Before she could say anything more, Chet found himself grabbed by the shoulder and pushed forcefully away from Stacy by none other than the drunken brute, Ben Thompson.

"You're tempted, are you, Stacy?" Ben crowed,

leering down at her. "How about being tempted to dance with me?"

"What do you think you're doing?" Stacy was shocked by his crude moves. She tried to get back to Chet.

But Ben stepped between them, blocking her way.

He took her by the arm in an unyielding grip as he told her, "Forget about him. I'm cutting in."

"Wait a minute, Thompson—" Chet began.

"Get out of here, Harrison. I want a dance with the fine lady from the Dollar," Ben declared.

"Stacy's my fiancée. She's with me," he challenged.

Ben wanted to fight more than he'd wanted to dance. He deliberately taunted Chet, "Get lost. She's mine.

"Ben Thompson, let me go!" Stacy fought to pull herself free of his painful grip. She knew what he was up to and wanted nothing to do with it.

The folks who were dancing nearby realized there was trouble brewing, and they quickly backed off and got out of the way.

"I ain't letting you go, Stacy. I done claimed you, and we're gonna dance. Right now," Ben ordered. He yanked her close and started to dance, knowing his actions would antagonize Chet even more.

"Thompson . . ." Chet wasn't about to let the drunken man get away with this. He went after him.

And that was just what Ben had been hoping for.

He was ready for Chet.

With savage force, he made his move, shoving Stacy aside and hitting Chet square in the jaw. The force of the blow sent Chet sprawling backward onto the floor.

"Chet!" Stacy cried out. She started to go to him, but Ben grabbed her by the arm again and held her back.

"Come on, little sugar, we gotta finish up our dance!"

Walker had been caught up in his dance with Roni when he heard his sister's cry and the musicians suddenly stopped playing. He turned just in time to see Ben standing triumphantly over the fallen Chet, his vile hands on Stacy.

Walker wasn't sure what had happened, but knowing Ben the way he did, he knew he had to get his sister away from him.

"Stay here," he ordered Roni.

Ben saw Walker coming and smiled to himself.

His plan had worked.

He had lured the half-breed in just like he'd wanted to.

Ben deliberately pulled Stacy close again, wanting to infuriate Walker even more, and he chuckled as he saw Chet trying to struggle to his feet.

"Come on, darlin', this is our dance. Musicians— why'd you quit playin'? Let's have us some music!" he ordered boisterously.

The musicians watched and waited nervously as Walker stalked over to confront Ben, with Jim following close behind.

"Get your hands off Stacy now, Thompson," Walker said quietly.

The whole room fell silent.

"Relax, we're just having a little fun." Ben sneered. "Your little sister wants to dance with me, don't ya, darlin'?" He tightened his hold on her threateningly.

Stacy refused to give in to his attempt to force her to his will. Hot-tempered as she was, she wasn't about to put up with his bullying ways. "You're the last man I'd ever want to dance with, Ben Thompson!"

A cowgirl born and bred, she wished she had her gun with her or, at least, had her boots on so she could kick him and get herself free. But dressed like a lady, she didn't have much hope of that. All she could do was try to twist her arm out of his bruising grip, and it wasn't working. Ben was too strong.

"Why, that ain't no way to talk to me, little darlin'," Ben snarled down at her.

"You heard Stacy," Walker dictated. "Let her go—now!"

"This is between me and Stacy. Right, honey? I don't take orders from anybody—least of all you." Ben looked at Walker and smiled thinly.

"You'd better start. Get away from my sister and stay off the Dollar!" Walker had long suspected him of rustling their cattle.

"What are you sayin', 'breed?" he challenged loudly. "Are you accusing me of somethin'?"

"I'm not accusing you of anything—I'm telling you. You set foot on the Dollar again and you'll pay the price!"

A murmur of tension went through the crowd. Rumors had flown for years about the bad blood between the two ranching families, and people feared things might be coming to a head right then.

Glad that he had Walker right where he wanted him, Ben made his move. He shoved Stacy straight at Chet, who had finally stood up, and then he lunged at Walker, throwing the first punch.

Chapter Three

*C*haos erupted.

Everyone in the hall panicked and rushed to get out of the way. They knew how dangerous Ben could be and feared the shooting might start at any minute.

Jim was ready to help Walker, but one of Ben's ranch hands forcefully grabbed him and held him back, and when Chet set Stacy aside to join in the fight, two of Ben's other men stopped him.

The fight was a fierce one.

Roni looked on in horror. She had never witnessed such a savage battle before. She was aware of the murmuring going through the crowd around her, and realized to her disgust that most of them were blaming Walker for the fight and hoping Ben would win, and that Ben's men were actually cheering him on. Wanting to do something to help, she hurried to Stacy to make sure she hadn't been injured.

"Did he hurt you?"

"No, no, I'm all right. I just wish I had my gun with me so I could break this up!"

Stacy was frantic as she looked around for something she could use as a weapon. She spotted some chairs pushed back against the wall and had just started to get one when Mark Davis, a deputy from town who was attending the dance, stepped in. He recruited some of the men in attendance to help him restrain Ben's ranch hands and break up the fight. It wasn't easy, but they finally managed to drag Ben and Walker apart.

"What do you want us to do with them?" one of the men asked as he struggled to hold on to Ben.

"Get them out of here!" Deputy Davis ordered, wanting to restore peace.

Ben and Walker were trying to break free, ready to go after each other again, but the other men forced them out through the front door. Ben was fighting so hard to get away, they had to physically throw him into the street to slow him down. Bloodied and furious, he landed heavily in the dirt and lay there glaring up at them. He was tempted to draw on them, but he was outnumbered.

"Get out of here, Thompson!" the deputy ordered as he went to stand over him, his hand resting threateningly on his gun. He had little use for the drunken, low-life rancher. Ben had been a source of trouble in the area for as long as Davis could remember. "Go sober up!"

Ben said nothing as he got to his feet and wiped the blood from the corner of his mouth. They might have thrown him .out of the dance, but he was already planning his next move. He cast one last glare Walker's way, threatening, "This ain't over, Stevenson."

"You're right. It's not," Walker replied, not backing down.

The drunk moved off into the night.

Deputy Davis turned to the men who were still restraining Walker.

"What do you want us to do with him?" they asked him.

"Let him go."

They did.

Walker stood there, waiting to hear what the deputy was going to say next.

"Go on back inside for now." The deputy knew there was a definite risk of more trouble if he didn't keep the two combatants separated.

Walker turned and was just starting back into the hall when Thompson's ranch hands came out to follow their boss. They exchanged threatening looks, but said nothing as they passed each other. They knew better than to trade barbs with the deputy standing right there.

"Where'd Ben go?" Mick asked Deputy Davis.

"To sober up. You boys should go do the same. I don't want any more trouble in town tonight or you'll all be waking up in jail tomorrow morning."

Grumbling, they moved off to find Ben and see what he wanted them to do next. They had a feeling, no matter what the deputy said, the fight wasn't over.

Walker entered the hall to find all the other people standing back, watching him suspiciously, and one of the men from town keeping the crowd restrained.

Deputy Davis followed him in and went up front to announce, "All the excitement's over, folks. Go on back to having a good time. Musicians, let's get some music going!"

The musicians did just that and the mood in the room relaxed a bit. The crowd of onlookers went back to enjoying themselves, although more than a few cast troubled looks Walker's way, clearly wondering why he hadn't been thrown out of the dance along with Ben Thompson.

Roni managed to reach Walker first, followed by Stacy, Chet and Jim. "Are you all right?"

"I'll live." He'd been in far worse fights over the years and was more concerned about his sister. He looked at Stacy. "How are you?"

"Fine, now that Ben's gone," she told him quickly.

"Good." He was glad she'd come to no harm at Ben's hands.

"That man is nothing but an animal," she said in disgust, remembering how horrible it had felt to have Ben's hands upon her.

"He won't be bothering you anymore," Walker promised, his tone serious.

"Where did he go?" Chet asked.

"Deputy Davis and the other men ran him off and told him to sober up."

"Good. We don't need any more trouble tonight," Jim remarked.

"We don't need his kind of trouble—ever," Stacy insisted. She looked up at her brother. "Walker?"

He gazed down at her and saw the concern in her eyes. "What?"

"Thank you."

He nodded, remembering the promise he'd made to their father on his deathbed to protect her and keep her safe.

"Come on, darling," Chet told Stacy. "Let's dance."

"I'd like that," she agreed, going into his arms.

Roni stayed with Walker as they moved off to the side of the room with Jim.

"Why did Ben Thompson deliberately want to pick a fight with you tonight?" Roni asked. Violent behavior always troubled her.

"He hates us because the Dollar is so successful. My father had trouble with him in the past. Before he died, he warned me that Ben might be behind some of the rustling that's been going on."

"Well, let's just hope Ben gets out of town and stays out of town for a while."

"That would be good. Real good, because I want to finish my dance with you."

Roni smiled up at him in delight. "That's right. We were interrupted, weren't we?"

He took her hand and led her out to join the other couples. When the music ended, they reluctantly started back to join Jim, and Roni noticed a woman standing with him, looking anxious and worried.

"Dr. Reynolds, I'm Polly Hathaway," the woman

began earnestly when she drew near. "I need your help. It's my son—"

"What's wrong?"

"He's started running a terrible fever—"

"Let's go see him right now," Roni offered without hesitation. She turned to Walker and Jim, regretfully telling them, "I have to go."

They said good-bye and watched as she hurried from the hall with the mother to tend to the sick young boy.

"I don't know about you, but I could use a drink right now," Jim said. "Why don't we head over to the Ace High?"

"That sounds good," Walker agreed. With Roni gone, he could see no reason to stay at the dance.

They made a quick exit, glad to get away.

On the far side of the hall, one of the young ladies from town, Christie Miller, was upset as she watched Walker leave with Jim.

"I can't believe it," Christie said in a disheartened tone as she looked at her friend, Sandra Welch. "I waited all night for the Ladies' Choice Dance, and when it's almost time, Walker leaves."

Sandra understood her friend's disappointment. Christie had been talking about the handsome rancher and wanting to dance with him all night long. Knowing Christie's parents as she did, though, Sandra realized Walker's leaving was probably the best thing that could have happened.

"There are a lot of other men here you can ask to dance when the time comes," Sandra told her.

"I know, but I wanted to dance with Walker. He's so—"

"Good-looking?"

"Yes," she agreed quickly, an image of the tall, lean, darkly handsome rancher going through her mind.

"But you have to remember what your father would say about your dancing with him. You know how he feels about Walker being a half-breed."

"I know, but he is a Stevenson and he's rich. That should count for something, wouldn't you think?"

"Not with your father it doesn't, and not with a lot of folks around town. They don't approve of Walker."

"I know you're right, but I was still hoping to get the chance." The fact that her parents disapproved of Walker had made him all the more exciting to Christie, but that didn't matter now that he was gone. Disappointed though she was, Christie started looking around the hall at all the eligible bachelors, planning her strategy for claiming a dance partner as soon the Ladies' Choice was announced.

Ben met up with his men in a dark alley on the far side of town.

"What are you going to do, Boss?" Mick asked. He knew Ben well enough to know his fight with the half-breed was far from over.

"Yeah, you can't let Walker get away with this!" another man added.

"You're right. He's not going to get away with it." The pain and humiliation Ben was feeling were driving him on. It had been bad enough that Walker had been getting the best of him in the fight at the dance, but then when the deputy had let the half-breed stay and had thrown him out, he'd been beyond furious. "I'm not through with him yet. I'm going to be there waiting for him when he heads over to the hotel. He told me I was going to 'pay the price,' but tonight, he's the one who's going to be paying up."

"But what if he's not alone?"

Ben turned a deadly look on the man who'd asked the question. "Then the people with him will learn a lesson about how to pick their friends."

"How soon do you think he'll be showing up?" Mick asked.

"I'm heading over there now. I only need a few of you with me. The rest of you can go on back to the ranch."

"Why don't you just shoot him and be done with it?" another ranch hand asked.

Ben laughed. "Shooting him would be too easy. I want him to feel this and remember it."

A few minutes later, Ben and the men who remained with him took the back way across town. They positioned themselves in the dark passageways in the area around the hotel to keep watch.

Chapter Four

Walker and Jim made their way to the Ace High and settled in at the bar. Even with the dance going on, the saloon was crowded.

"What'll it be?" Antonio, the bartender, asked as he came to wait on them.

"Whiskey," they both answered.

"I heard talk there was some trouble over at the dance tonight," Antonio said as he set their glasses before them on the bar, then quickly filled them up with the potent liquor.

"News travels fast around here," Walker remarked, and took a deep drink. "What did you hear?"

"I heard you were getting the best of Ben until the deputy stepped in and broke things up."

"Yes, he was," Jim agreed. "Ben showed up at the dance just looking for a fight tonight and he got one."

"I had that feeling when he left here. He and his boys had been drinking for quite a while and they were getting mean before they headed over to the dance. We were real glad to see them go."

"Let's just hope they don't come back," commented Brenda Wagner, a dark-haired, sultry saloon girl who joined them.

"Deputy Davis ordered Ben to get out of town," Walker told them.

"That's the best news I've heard all night," Brenda remarked. She'd been worrying about herself and the other girls if the rancher and his men came back. They'd been known to get rough some nights. Brenda was smiling as she looked Walker and Jim over with open interest. She purred, "If you two need anything, anything at all, just let me know."

"We will," Jim promised her as she moved off to work the rest of the room.

They got refills on their drinks and went to sit at one of the tables in the back of the bar to relax for a while.

It was getting late when Walker and Jim left the saloon. Jim lived in a small house at the end of town, past the hotel where Walker and Stacy had taken rooms for the night, so they headed that way together.

Ben and the three hands who'd stayed in town with him were ready and waiting. At first, they weren't sure who was with Walker as he approached, but when they saw it was only the banker, they weren't worried. Jim might be tall, but they knew he wasn't much of a fighter, and they believed he would be easy to take down.

Walker and Jim were just coming up on the hotel when Walker sensed something wasn't right. He stopped and looked around, frowning into the night.

"Did you hear something?" he asked Jim.

"No—"

Jim didn't get the chance to say anything more. Ben and his boys rushed them from out of the shadows. Caught off guard and outnumbered as they were, Walker and Jim were dragged back into the alleyway, and the brutal fight was on.

Jim put up a good fight, but one of Ben's men hit him savagely on the head from behind and knocked him unconscious. He collapsed and lay unmoving on the ground as Walker continued to try to hold his own. Even though he was a fierce fighter, Walker was no match for the four men teamed up against him. With his ranch hands keeping Walker restrained, Ben beat him mercilessly.

"Thought I'd do what the deputy told me to do, did you? Thought I'd just ride out of town and not look back?" Ben took great pleasure in taunting Walker as he hit him. "Well, think again—half-breed! I'm going to take care of you, and then I just may go after that pretty little Reynolds girl you were so hot for tonight."

Walker was furious that Ben would dare to speak of Roni that way. "Leave Roni out of this!"

"Well, did you hear that, boys? I think the 'breed here has something going with the new doc in town. And if she likes you, she'll really like me and the boys—won't she, fellas?"

The men all hooted in agreement with him.

"Yeah, she's so pretty, we won't mind too much that your filthy hands have been on her. I bet she's a wild one to ride—what do you think, boys?"

His men laughed and continued to make lewd comments about Roni as Walker fought desperately to break loose.

Walker wanted to defend Roni's honor, but Ben kept beating him. Pain jarred Walker as he felt his ribs crack. He sagged against their brutal restraint while Ben continued his abuse.

Chet and Stacy had been enjoying themselves to the fullest at the dance, and they were sorry when the evening came to an end.

"When will I get to see you again?" Stacy asked him as they left the hall and made their way to the hotel.

"I'll try to make it over to the Dollar next weekend."

"You know, you don't have to ride home tonight. You could spend the night here. I'm sure they've got extra rooms available at the hotel, and then you could go home tomorrow," she said hopefully, wanting to spend as much time with him as she could. "We could go to church and have breakfast together."

"I have to get back," he told her regretfully.

"Are you sure?"

"You know there's nothing I'd like more than to stay in town longer with you, but I can't—not this trip."

He drew her into the darkness to steal a quick kiss, and then they moved on toward the hotel. Chet kept a possessive arm around her as he escorted her inside the lobby. He bid her good night and watched her until she'd started up the stairs before taking his leave.

Chet went back outside and stood there for a moment, smiling broadly into the night. Things in his life were finally going good—real good. And now that Stacy was out of the way, he could do what he really wanted to do—and that wasn't ride for home.

The Ace High was calling him, and so was a pretty little gal named Suzie.

He paid regular visits to the buxom, dark-haired beauty, and she was expecting him tonight. He was looking forward to being with her. She really knew how to please a man. He started off eagerly in the direction of the saloon.

Chet hadn't gotten very far when he heard what sounded like a fight between some of the buildings near the hotel. He hurried over to see what was happening. He was shocked to find Jim lying unconscious and bloodied on the ground, and Ben's men restraining Walker while Ben pummeled him brutally.

Chet was stunned by the fact that his future brother-in-law couldn't seem to come into town without ending up in trouble. First, the fight at the dance and now this . . .

Chet wanted to run, but he knew he couldn't. He could tell Walker couldn't take much more beating, and since he was marrying Stacy for the Stevenson money, he was going to have to help Walker—whether he wanted to or not.

But even if he went to Walker's aid, Chet knew they were still outnumbered. There was only one way he could stop the carnage. He drew his gun and stepped forward to confront Ben and his men.

"Let him go and back off!" he ordered in a loud voice.

Ben was startled by the unexpected order. Seeing that it was only Chet standing there, he started to go for his gun, but Chet was ready. He got off a shot, hitting the ground right in front of Ben and stopping him cold in his tracks.

"I said back off!" Chet repeated.

"Who the hell do you think you are?" Ben snarled.

"I'm the man who's holding a gun on you—that's who I am," Chet returned. "Now, let Walker go before you force me to use this!"

"We outnumber you."

Chet stayed calm as he coolly replied, "Yes, you do, and one of your boys might be able to get my gun away from me, but not before I end your miserable life."

"Why you—" Ben seethed.

"Let Walker go and get out of here while you still can. I'm not going to ask again."

Ben was furious, but knew there would be another time to deal with Chet; a time when Chet didn't have the upper hand. "Let's go, boys."

The ranch hands wasted no time. They threw Walker violently to the ground and took off with Ben into the night.

Once he was certain they were gone, Chet raced to Walker's side. He took one last look around before holstering his gun.

Walker was on his hands and knees in the dirt.

"Walker, let me help you." Chet pulled him to his feet.

Walker swayed unsteadily for a moment, but he immediately looked around for his friend. "Where's Jim?"

"He's over there."

They hurried to check on Jim and found he was still unconscious. In the dark of the alley, it was difficult to tell how serious his injuries were.

"He needs help. We'd better get him over to Roni's," Walker said.

They managed to support his weight between them, and they started over to the doctor's office a few blocks away.

Chet was furious as he helped get the unconscious Jim to the office. Suzie was waiting for him. He realized Jim was badly injured, but that had nothing to do with him. He was beginning to regret ever setting his sights on marrying Stacy, for it meant he was going to have to deal with Walker for the rest of his life.

After leaving the dance with the frantic mother, Roni had hurried to the office to get her medicine bag and then had gone straight to the woman's home to tend to the sick little boy. A sense of fear and dread had filled her, for a high fever could be a symptom of several dangerous diseases, diphtheria being one of them. She still remembered how, some years before, her father had tried to help a family stricken with diphtheria. Despite his best efforts, six of the family's seven children had suffocated from the horrible disease within days of each other.

When Roni had arrived at the home, she'd found the boy's fever to be dangerously high, but she'd been relieved to discover there was no inflamed diphtheritic membrane in his throat, threatening to block his windpipe. She had given the child some willow bark tea to drink and then after a tepid bath, had wiped him down with alcohol to lower his fever. It had taken some time, but once he'd finally been resting more comfortably, she'd returned home to her rooms above the office to get some sleep.

Roni had gone to bed, knowing she'd done all she could to help the sick boy. As she'd tried to relax, her thoughts had gone to the events of the night just past and sleep had proven elusive. She'd found herself thinking about dancing with Walker and then the ugliness of the fight with Ben. She remembered all her parents' warnings about not having anything to do with Walker Stevenson. They'd warned her that he was a half-breed and a savage. Even so, she hadn't ever thought of him as savage, not even during the fight. During his confrontation with Ben, she'd thought of him as fearless and brave.

A sudden, unexpected pounding at the office door below startled her; from the urgency of the pounding, she knew it had to be an emergency. Jumping out of bed, she quickly got dressed. She remembered how many times when she was a child her family had been awakened in the middle of the night by folks in dire trouble, and she wanted to be ready to help them, just as her father had been.

"Roni! It's Walker! Hurry! Jim has been hurt!" Walker called out to her when he finally heard her moving around inside.

Roni did just that. She quickly lit a lamp and started down the narrow staircase to the main floor to let them in. She hurriedly unlocked the door and threw it wide to find Chet and Walker standing there, supporting the unconscious Jim between them, one of his arms around each of their shoulders.

"What happened?" she asked as they carefully maneuvered him into the office and managed to lay him down on the examining table in the back room. "Has he been shot?"

"No," Walker answered tersely. "Ben and some of his men jumped us in the back alley. Jim didn't stand a chance."

Roni lit another lamp, washed her hands and began to examine Jim's injuries. Then she glanced up at Walker, who was standing nearby with Chet, bloody and obviously in some pain.

"What about you?" she asked, concerned.

"Don't worry about me," he said dismissively. "Take care of Jim."

"All right. Here." She got several clean towels and handed them to him. "You two can go wait out front."

"No," Walker refused. He wasn't going anywhere. "It's my fault this happened to him. I'm staying."

"Do you want me to go tell Stacy?" Chet asked Walker.

"No. There's no need." There would be time to tell her of the fight tomorrow. Right at this moment, all that mattered was Jim.

Chet nodded and left the room. He closed the door behind him. He was thoroughly disgusted as he sat down heavily in one of the two wooden chairs to wait.

He really wanted to leave.

He didn't care about the banker.

He wanted to get over to the Ace High.

Suzie was expecting him.

Not that he could let anyone know what he was thinking. He had to play his part, but he was beginning to wonder how long he would be able to keep up the charade once he and Stacy got married. It'd be interesting, that was for sure. He was going to find out just how good an actor he really was.

Chet stared out the office window into the night, wondering how long he was going to be stuck there.

Roni felt Jim's scalp for any swelling and then, holding the lamp close, lifted his eyelids one at a time to check his pupils' response to light. She was relieved when their response seemed normal. Carefully, she bandaged his head injury.

"How is he?" Walker asked. "Is he going to be OK?"

She looked up at him, her expression serious as she told him honestly, "I don't think he has a concussion, but I won't know for sure until he regains consciousness."

"Is there anything more you can do?"

"The only thing we can do right now is wait." She went over to Walker, watching him closely. He'd wiped the blood from his face, but she could tell he'd taken quite a beating. "Let's get your shirt off. The way you're moving, I think you may have some broken ribs."

From the pain he was in, Walker knew she was right. He unbuttoned his shirt and started to painfully shrug out of it.

Roni stepped up to help him finish getting it off. She had known he was a fine specimen of manhood, and seeing him partially unclothed this way left no doubt of his masculinity. She frowned as she saw the savage bruises already darkening his skin, and her touch was gentle on his broad, muscular chest and back as she examined him. Walker remained stoic as she worked on him. He didn't utter a sound as she tightly bound his chest, but she could see that his jaw was locked against the pain that was racking him from his cracked ribs.

"There, that should hold," she told him as she finished. "You need to get some rest now."

"I told you, I'm not going anywhere until I know how Jim is." Walker got up and shrugged back into his shirt as he watched his friend. "Why did they have to do this to him? I was the one they were after."

"Are you going to go get the sheriff or Deputy Davis?"

"No."

He looked down at her, and the fierce emotions she saw in his eyes frightened her.

"Ben Thompson's going to pay for what he's done! He's gonna pay."

The tone of his voice and the threat in his words sent a chill of foreboding through her.

Chet knocked quietly on the closed door then, and Roni went to open it.

"Is there anything I can do?" He had heard what Walker had just said, and he looked past the two of them to where Jim still lay unmoving.

"No," Walker told him. "There's no reason for you to stay, too."

"Are you sure? I can go get Stacy and—"

"Go on home. I'll tell Stacy what happened in the morning."

"You'll let me know how Jim is?"

"I'll send word. And Chet?" Walker met his gaze straight on. "Thanks."

Chet nodded and left the office, deep in thought. Because it was so late, he decided to walk to the stable to get his horse and then ride over to the Ace High from there. He still had something important to take care of: Suzie.

After retrieving his horse, he made his way to the saloon and tied up around back so no one would see him. Confident no one had noticed his arrival, he knocked on the back door.

"I've been waiting for you!" Suzie said as she let him in.

"Good." He grabbed the voluptuous beauty and

kissed her hungrily, openly groping her lush curves. "Let's get upstairs."

"You're in a hurry tonight."

"You're right. I am."

"What about your sweet little Stacy?" she asked hatefully. "Doesn't she know how to please a man?"

"Not like you do," he said, leering at her as they hurried up the steps together.

Chet wasted no time once they'd locked themselves in her room. He threw her on the bed and lifted her skirts, eager to have his way with her.

Suzie was used to his wild ways and matched him in his driving passion. It didn't take them long to slake their desire.

Chapter Five

Roni finished checking on Jim again and then went into the outer office to find Walker standing there in silence with his back to her, staring out the window into the darkness. She paused for a moment to study him. He was a powerful presence, so tall and strong.

For a moment, Roni could see the fierce warrior who lived deep within the heart of him, that part of himself he kept so carefully hidden from everyone. It was the warrior who had saved her and Jim's dog all those years ago; the warrior who had rescued Stacy tonight from Ben Thompson's drunken abuse and had battled him on the dance floor. A shiver of sensual recognition trembled through her.

Without speaking, she went to stand beside him.

Walker had sensed her presence as soon as she had appeared in the doorway. He turned to her. "Has there been any change?"

"No, not yet."

His expression darkened even more. He said nothing for a moment as he looked back out the window again into the blackness of the night. He almost felt as if he were gazing into the depths of his own soul. Ben's vile words about Roni echoed in his thoughts, haunting him, and he knew he had to warn her.

"Roni, I want you to stay away from Ben Thompson. After the way he acted tonight, I wouldn't put anything past him."

"Do you think he's still in town?"

"I hope not, but there's no way of knowing."

Roni went to the door and secured the lock, then pulled down the window shade so no one could see in to the office. "There. Just in case he is still around."

She was standing close to him and started to move away, but he reached out to draw her back to him. He gazed down at her, seeing her beauty and kindness.

"Good," he said softly. "I want you safe."

"Oh, Walker—"

There was no need for either one of them to say more. He kissed her. His mouth moved over hers in a sensual, possessive caress that left her breathless.

When the kiss ended, Roni stayed there in his arms and treasured his nearness and his strength. It surprised her that after all he'd been through that night, he was worried about her safety. She wanted him to be safe, too.

"Are you sure you don't want to let the sheriff

know what happened?" she asked, looking up at Walker.

Remembering the ugly threats Ben had made about Roni, Walker answered, "I'm sure."

"But he could go after Ben and his men, and arrest them. Then you wouldn't have to worry—"

"What happened with Ben tonight was personal. I'll handle it." He stepped back and moved away from her. He needed to distance himself from her so he could think clearly.

She sensed the sudden change in his mood and heard the steel in his voice, and knew there was nothing more she could say to make him change his mind.

"I'd better go back in with Jim."

Walker followed her to maintain his vigil by his friend's side.

Chet collapsed back on the bed, smiling. Suzie sure knew how to please a man.

Suzie stretched out next to him and ran a seductive hand over his bare chest.

"I wish you could stay longer," she said huskily. He always paid her handsomely.

"I wish I could, too, believe me. There's nothing I'd like better than to spend a few days and nights locked up in this room with you."

"Your little fiancée would miss you," she taunted.

"What she doesn't know . . ."

"Does she please you like I do?" Suzie had to admit she was envious of the other woman—to be so rich and to have Chet, too.

"Nobody pleases me like you do," he told her, pulling her beneath him for another heated coupling.

And Suzie earned her pay.

Less than an hour later, Chet was on his way out of town. As he thought about all that had happened that night, he realized that this was his chance to get what he really wanted: the Dollar Ranch all for his own. During the course of his time with Suzie, he had told her about breaking up the fight, and she had mentioned that some of Ben's hands had come into the saloon to drink not long before he'd shown up. When the bartender had asked where Ben was, the ranch hands had said he'd already left town.

Chet smiled to himself.

This was the perfect opportunity.

In a matter of months, he'd be married to Stacy, and if he found a way to use this fight with Ben Thompson to get rid of Walker, things would be perfect.

All he had to do was figure out how to pull it off.

Instead of going to his own ranch, Chet rode toward the Thompson place.

Walker was sitting in a chair next to the table where Jim lay, his head resting in his hands, when Jim gave a low groan and began to stir.

"Roni!" Walker got up and rushed to the doorway to let her know Jim was coming around.

She hurried back into the room and was relieved to find her patient was regaining consciousness.

"What the—" Jim muttered as awareness returned, and with it near blinding pain. He lifted one hand to his aching head.

"Easy, Jim." Roni was by his side in an instant. "Don't try to move or do anything too fast."

He opened his eyes and struggled to focus on Roni and Walker, who were standing over him. It took a moment for him to figure out where he was and what must have happened. When he did, he groaned even louder.

"Now, I remember." He looked over at Walker. "It was Thompson, wasn't it?"

"Yes. He and his men were waiting for us," Walker answered. "How do you feel?"

"Like hell," Jim muttered, trying to sit up.

"Just stay where you are," Roni ordered and held him down. Beat up and weak as he was, it wasn't difficult for her.

"Yes, Doc," Jim answered obediently with a wry, pained grin. He knew she was right. Just that small effort had left him dizzy and hurting all over.

She knew that smile and was glad to see Jim truly was himself again. "That's more like it. You can try to sit up in a few minutes, but there's no need to rush it. When you do, you're going to feel it."

"I feel it already. How'd the fight get broken up?" Jim asked, looking over at Walker. "Did the deputy show up?"

"No, Chet did." Walker went on to explain how his future brother-in-law had appeared just in time and had run Ben and his men off.

"Good thing Chet came along when he did." Jim

didn't like to be beholden to the other man, but he knew he owed him a big debt.

"You're right about that." There was no telling what Ben and his men might have done if they hadn't been interrupted.

Walker hadn't fully buttoned his shirt and Jim could see the bandages around his chest. "How bad are you?"

"Just a couple of cracked ribs. Roni took care of it."

Jim looked at Roni. "In case he hasn't told you, we're real glad you're back in town. You're a good doc."

"You had doubts?" she teased him.

"Never."

"Should I try to get him home?" Walker asked her.

"It would be best for him to stay here in the office overnight."

Jim offered no protest. The way he was feeling, he knew he needed to stay right where he was.

"While he's here, I'll be close by in case there's any kind of complication with his head injury. We'll know more in the morning about how capable he is of moving around on his own."

"All right. I'll come back then," Walker said. He looked down at his friend, relieved that Jim's injuries weren't as serious as he'd feared. "I'll see you tomorrow."

Jim could only give a slight nod.

Roni walked Walker to the door so she could lock up after him. Walker had just started outside when she spoke. "Walker."

He looked back at her questioningly, and she went straight into his arms and kissed him. He held her close and kissed her deeply before putting her from him reluctantly.

"Be careful," she said, gazing up at him.

"You, too." He gave her one last tender kiss before leaving her.

Walker waited until he was certain she'd locked the office door before moving off. It was late and he was glad the streets were deserted.

Walker reached the hotel and found the clerk was nowhere in sight. That was fine with him. He wanted nothing to do with anyone right then. He went on up to his room and gingerly shed his shirt. His chest was hurting so much, he didn't even think about trying to undress more than that. He stretched out on the bed and sought what comfort he could, but sleep proved elusive. His thoughts kept returning to Ben Thompson and how he was going to find a way to teach him a lesson once and for all. It was only as the early morning hours came that he finally managed to fall asleep.

Ben was feeling pleased with himself as he rode through the night. It wasn't often that he enjoyed himself so much in town, but this had been a mighty entertaining trip, that was for sure. He'd been looking forward to having a good time, and it didn't get any better than taking on Walker Stevenson—and winning. The filthy half-breed . . .

Ben smiled to himself at the memory of the fight in the alley. Everything had worked out just fine. His men had backed him up when he'd needed them most, so he'd left them behind to enjoy themselves at the saloon. He was certain they wouldn't head back to the ranch until the next afternoon, but that was all right. They'd earned a night of carousing.

Ben's thoughts turned to Walker. It was too bad the banker had been with the 'breed, but Jim should have known better than to deal with his kind. Walker had put up a good fight, but he'd been no match for him and his men. In the end, they'd given him quite a beating. The prospect of how badly the 'breed was going to be hurting in the morning pleased Ben. It was just a damn shame that Chet had shown up.

Still, Ben continued smiling.

He'd beaten the half-breed in the fight tonight, and that was all that mattered to him.

Ben hadn't been riding fast, and he knew he wasn't going to make it all the way back to his ranch tonight. Ready to bed down for the night, he found a spot to make his camp. He built a small fire and spread out his bedroll before tending to his horse and getting his flask from his saddlebag. He settled in, enjoying some more whiskey before finally passing out.

It was much later when Chet caught sight of the low-burning campfire off in the distance. Taking great care not to make a sound, he dismounted and made his way toward the site on foot, armed with his rifle. He'd been hoping he would get lucky, and as he got close enough to see who was bedded down there, he knew he had.

It was none other than Ben Thompson.

And he was sound asleep.

Cold-blooded man that he was, Chet did what he'd come to do. Ben never had a chance as the sound of the single gunshot echoed eerily through the silence of the night. Chet knew enough people had witnessed the fight at the dance to suspect Walker right away. Satisfied his plan was perfect, Chet returned to his horse and rode for his own ranch.

Soon, very soon, he was going to have everything he'd ever wanted.

Stacy was sorry that Chet hadn't decided to stay in town and attend church with her that morning, but she still hoped to get Walker to go. She rose early and got ready, wearing her Sunday best. Walker was usually up at dawn, so when she didn't hear him moving around in his room, she wondered if he'd already gone down to the stable to get the buckboard hitched up and the horses ready for the trip home. She hurried downstairs to see if she could find him.

"Good morning, Miss Stacy," said Lester, the clerk.

"Good morning," she returned. "Have you seen my brother yet this morning?"

"No, ma'am, I haven't, but I've only been at the desk for the last half hour or so."

"Thanks, Lester."

Stacy considered going to the stable to look for him, but decided to wait at the hotel since she was already dressed in her nice clothes. She went back upstairs and was just passing by Walker's room when the door opened and he stepped out into the hall.

"There you are—" She stopped, shocked by the sight of his bruised jaw. "Walker! What happened to you?"

"I'll tell you all about it on the way over to Roni's office."

"Roni's office? Why do we have to go there this morning?"

"Come on." He took her arm, and they went down to the lobby.

"So he was upstairs after all, was he?" the clerk remarked as they passed through.

"Yes, he was," Stacy told him, forcing herself to smile as she let Walker usher her from the building. "All right," she demanded in a low voice. "Tell me everything! Now! What's going on?"

Walker told her what had happened and how Chet had shown up just in time to run Ben and his men off and save him from further harm.

"That must have been right after he dropped me off at the hotel."

"They'd knocked Jim unconscious, so Chet helped me get him over to Roni's."

"How bad is Jim hurt?" She cared about Jim and feared he'd been badly injured.

"He came around, but Roni insisted he spend the night there with her so she could keep an eye on him."

"What about you?" She could tell he wasn't moving with his usual ease.

He shrugged. "Roni patched me up. I'll be all right."

"Why didn't you come and get me?" she demanded, wishing she'd been there to help in some way. "I could have done something—"

"There was nothing you could do. There was nothing any of us could do until Jim regained consciousness. Once he came around and started talking, he seemed like himself again, but I don't know if he'll be up and moving yet."

"And you didn't go tell the sheriff about this?"

"No. I trust Sheriff Protzel, but I didn't want to get the law involved. This is between Ben and me."

Stacy put any thoughts of going to church that morning aside. She was worried about Jim and wanted to make sure he was all right.

They reached Roni's office and knocked softly on the door.

Roni answered it quickly and let them in. They noticed immediately that the door to the back room was closed, so they kept their voices down.

"Roni, Walker just told me what happened. How is Jim?" Stacy asked worriedly.

"How was he during the night?" Walker added.

"He only stirred a few times. Otherwise, he rested quietly. It might take a day or two for him to get his strength back, but he should make a full recovery."

Walker and Stacy were both relieved by the good news.

"When can we talk to him?" Walker asked.

"Let me check if he's awake."

Roni opened the door to check on Jim and found he was stirring.

"Well, good morning," she greeted him as she went on in. "Walker and Stacy are here to see you."

Jim frowned, suddenly feeling self-conscious about being in such bad shape. He didn't want Stacy to see him this way. He wanted to get up and act as if he was fine. Determined to try to act unhurt, he swung his long legs over the side of the table and tried to push himself into a sitting position. A strong wave of dizziness and nausea swept over him, though, and he was forced to lean forward and rest his head in his hands as he fought for control.

Stacy hurried to his side and put a comforting hand on his shoulder. "Are you all right?"

Roni was there, too. "Like I told you, you're going to have to take it nice and easy for a while, Jim. Don't try to make any sudden moves. That'll only make things worse."

"How long is this going to last?" he asked, looking up at Roni. Even though he felt disoriented, he was all too aware of Stacy's presence beside him and her gentle touch upon him.

"It should pass in a day or two."

"And until it does, I'm going to stay right here in town and keep an eye on you," Stacy said.

"That's not necessary," Jim protested. It wasn't that he didn't want to spend time with Stacy. There was nothing he wanted more, loving her as he did, but it was humiliating enough just having her there with him now.

"You think I can't tell how bad you're hurting?"

Stacy challenged, using the same tone on him that she used on Walker when she was determined to have her way. "You live alone. What if you needed something and there was nobody around to help you?"

"I'll be all right," he insisted. He was used to taking care of himself.

"That's right. You will be, because I'm going to be nursing you."

"There's no point in arguing with her, Jim," Walker advised him with a wry smile, knowing how determined his sister could be when she made up her mind to do something.

Jim knew Walker was right. He was definitely losing the argument, so he managed a half-grin at her. "So, are you thinking about giving up ranching and taking up doctoring like Roni?"

"I just might. You never know," Stacy retorted, daring him to say more.

"That's a good idea. I could use the help," Roni said, smiling. She looked at Jim. "You listen to Stacy and do what she says. I'll come by your house and check on you, too, just to make sure you're behaving yourself."

"I'll keep my room over at the hotel, then," Stacy said.

"There's no need. I've got an extra bedroom upstairs. You're welcome to stay here with me, if you'd like," Roni offered.

"Thank you. I appreciate it."

"Let's see about getting Jim back home now,"

Roni began. "Once he's settled in and comfortable, we can go fetch your things from the hotel."

"That'll be fine."

Roni looked at Walker. "How are you holding up? Did you get any rest last night?"

"Not much, but I'll be all right."

"That's good to know," Stacy quipped, hoping to lighten their moods a little.

"I had a good doctor," he told them, his gaze warm upon Roni.

"Are you going to stay in town or go back home?" Stacy asked.

"I'll help you get Jim over to his house, and then I'd better head back."

"I'll send word if there is any change in his condition," Roni said, and then looked at Jim. "You are looking better this morning, so I think you'll be back to normal in a day or two."

"Like Walker said," Jim put in, "I have a real good doctor."

"Yeah, the new doc in town knows what she's doing," Stacy added.

"I'm just doing my job," Roni countered with a laugh.

"Your father would be proud of you," Stacy told her.

Chapter Six

Jim knew he wasn't a physically strong man. The fight last night had proven that to him yet another time, but through the years, what he'd lacked in physical strength, he'd made up for by outsmarting those he came up against. He'd been successful in his banking career, and he'd always believed he had the intelligence and strength of character to make the best of any difficult situation that might befall him.

That was until now.

The prospect of having Stacy at his house with him for the next few days was like his wildest dream coming true, but it was also going to put his inner strength to the test. Not to mention the fact that he was indebted to Chet now for helping to save his life and she was engaged to the rancher.

Yet despite the dilemma he found himself in, Jim had to smile. If being in the fight was what it had taken to get a chance to spend time alone with Stacy, it had been worth it.

"You're smiling," Stacy remarked, coming to stand in the parlor doorway to look at him lying on the sofa. "You must be feeling better."

The strain of just making the short trip from Roni's office to his home had left him pale and a bit shaken, and Roni had insisted that he rest and not try to move around too much for the remainder of the day. Stacy was glad to see he was following doctor's orders so far.

"I am," Jim told her. "You're here."

She laughed, believing he was teasing her. "Are you getting hungry? I thought I'd start fixing dinner soon."

She hoped he'd get his appetite back, for he'd barely eaten anything that day. Roni had told her that a head injury could sometimes cause nausea and loss of appetite.

"You know, I am getting a little hungry."

"Good. Do you feel up to sitting in the kitchen with me and keeping me company while I cook?"

"Sure." He started to try to stand.

"Here—let me help you."

Stacy went to his side and slipped a supportive arm about his lean waist as he got to his feet.

Jim enjoyed her sweet scent and the warmth of her body pressed against him as they made their way slowly from the parlor. He almost wished it was a longer walk to the kitchen.

"Roni said she'd be coming by a little later to look in on you again, so maybe she'll stay and eat with us."

"That would be good. I didn't get much of a chance to thank her for taking care of me the way she did."

"We're blessed to have her, that's for sure. After her father died, I wondered if we'd ever get another doc in town."

They moved into the kitchen and Jim sat at the table while Stacy began to prepare the meal.

It was late afternoon when Mick and the other ranch hands who'd spent the night in town made it back to the Thompson ranch. Mick left his horse down at the stable and went up to the house to let Ben know they'd returned.

"Where's the boss?" he asked Maria, the housekeeper, when she came to the door to let him in.

Maria gave him a strange look. "He's not here. I thought he stayed in town with you."

"No, he rode out last night. He said he was coming home then."

"He never showed up. I haven't seen him."

Mick frowned. Hungover as he was, the last thing he felt like doing was riding out again, but he had no choice. "Something must have gone wrong. We'd better go look for him."

He went back down to the stable to give the other men the news. They weren't happy, but mounted up again and split into groups to search for their missing boss. They figured Ben's horse had thrown a shoe or gone lame, and Ben was trying to make his way back to the ranch on foot.

Mick and a ranch hand named Al had been

combing the land for hours, looking for some sign of their boss, when they heard the sound of gunfire in the distance. Mitch knew that was a signal that some of the other hands had found Ben, and he breathed a sigh of relief. It had been a long day.

They rode in the direction of the shots, but what they found when they reached the others shocked them.

"The boss is dead!" one of the men yelled when he saw them coming.

"He didn't have a chance! Whoever did this shot him down in cold blood!" another added.

Mick reined in and quickly dismounted to check on Ben. He was cursing under his breath when he stood up. It was obvious Ben had been asleep when he'd been killed.

Mick looked at the other men. "We still got some hours of daylight left. Spread out and take a look around. See if you can find anything that'll give us a clue who did this."

"We already know who did it!" one of the other men charged. "It was the half-breed!"

"It had to be! He threatened the boss at the dance! We all heard him!"

Mick thought they were right. "All right. Let's get Ben into town. We gotta let the sheriff know what happened."

They loaded up Ben's body and started the trek to town to notify the sheriff.

It was Sunday evening, and things usually stayed pretty quiet around town, so when Sheriff Protzel heard the commotion outside in the street, he got up from his desk to see what was going on. He walked out of the office to find Mick and several of the other men from the Thompson ranch tying up their horses out front. Strapped on the back of one of the horses was a dead body.

"Who is it? What happened?" the lawman asked, immediately going to grab the reins of the horse carrying the dead man.

"It's Ben, Sheriff!" Mick told him. "When he didn't make it back to the ranch today, we went looking for him. We found him at a campsite—shot dead."

Sheriff Protzel's expression grew even more grim as he inspected the body and saw how Ben had been shot.

"And none of you saw or heard anything?"

"No. We stayed in town all night. Ben went home on his own after the dance, but he never made it back to the ranch. We went looking for him today and found him at his campsite. Whoever did this shot him in cold blood while he was sleeping."

"And we know who did it!" one of the ranch hands told him.

"Yeah. It had to be Walker Stevenson! He's the one Ben fought with at the dance," another man put it.

"Did you find any evidence that it was Walker?" the lawman demanded.

"Ben's dead—what more evidence do you need?" Mick challenged.

"It was the half-breed. We all know it!" another ranch hand added.

"Yeah," Mick said, his tone threatening. "And if

you don't arrest him, we'll take care of him ourselves."

"Now, slow down there, boys," the sheriff cautioned them, resting his hand on his gun to let them know he meant business.

"No, you listen to us, Sheriff. That half-breed is a murderer! He killed Ben just as sure as we're standing here."

"Get Ben over to the undertaker's," Sheriff Protzel ordered, "and then come back here to the office. I don't want any of you running off doing something crazy. I'm the law in this town, and don't you forget it." His tone was harsh and his meaning unmistakable.

The men were grumbling as they backed down for the time being and did what the lawman ordered. They were willing to follow his direction for now, but if he didn't go after Walker, they would.

Sheriff Protzel watched them move away and then went straight over to Deputy Davis's house.

"We've got trouble," Protzel told his deputy when he came to the door.

"What is it?" Deputy Davis asked.

The sheriff told him what he knew.

"That fight at the dance was ugly," the deputy told him, "but Ben started the whole thing."

"I don't trust Thompson's men. They're a wild enough bunch to try just about anything. We'd better ride out and bring Walker in right now before things get out of hand. I wouldn't put it past them to try to lynch him."

"Let's get some more men to ride with us, just in case the Thompson boys do start some trouble."

Deputy Davis grabbed his gun belt and strapped it on before leaving the house.

A short time later, they were riding out to the Dollar, and three newly appointed deputies were accompanying them.

In town, Mick and the other men from the ranch awaited their return.

Walker had just been ready to call it a night when he heard riders coming in. It was highly unusual for anyone to show up this late, so he went outside to see who it was. He was puzzled to find Sheriff Protzel and several of his deputies riding up to the house.

" 'Evening, Sheriff." Walker greeted him cordially, going forward to speak with the men as they reined in. "Is something wrong?"

Sheriff Protzel dismounted, as did his deputies. His expression was serious as he faced Walker. "Walker, I need to talk with you—privately. There's been some trouble."

Walker realized something terrible must have happened as he looked from the lawman to his deputies, and he immediately worried that it had something to do with Stacy. "What is it? Is Stacy all right?"

The lawman knew no way of making this easy. "Can we go inside and talk?"

"Come in." Walker led the way into the house.

Before following Walker inside, Sheriff Protzel

paused and looked at his men, who were more than ready to come with him just in case there was trouble. "Wait out here. I won't be long."

Walker moved into the parlor to face the lawman, unsure of what was to come. "What's happened?"

"Ben Thompson is dead," the Sheriff said bluntly, and he watched Walker carefully, wanting to judge his reaction to the news.

"What?" Walker exclaimed in a shocked tone.

Sheriff Protzel was glad to see Walker looked honestly surprised by the news. "He didn't show up back at his ranch, so some of his boys went looking for him. They found him murdered at his campsite."

"What's this got to do with me?"

"I'm afraid I have to take you in."

"I don't understand." Of all the things Walker had thought he was going to say, this was the furthest from his mind. "You think I killed him?"

"Look, you two were involved in a fight at the dance and you did threaten him."

"I didn't do it," Walker protested. "I was in town last night. You can ask Stacy or Jim or even Roni. They'll tell you. I had a room at the hotel. I spent the night there."

"I'll check into that, but for now, I'm taking you in."

"If you're going to be arresting anybody, you should be arresting Ben's men," Walker argued angrily. "Ben and I did have a fight at the dance, all right, but later, Ben and some of his boys jumped Jim and me by the hotel. Jim spent the night in the doctor's office, he was beat up so bad."

"Walker, that just makes things look even worse for you," Sheriff Protzel told him.

"I didn't kill him," he repeated.

"I want to believe you, but until I get this sorted out, I'm going to keep you in custody. Ben's men are just waiting for the chance to lynch you, and I'm not going to let that happen. So, let's go."

Walker was disgusted, but he knew Sheriff Protzel was a fair and honest man. He knew it would be for the best if he went along without a fight.

"I need to tell my men what's going on," he said.

He'd just started outside when he saw his foreman, Zach Foster, being kept away from the house by the deputies.

"Walker, is everything all right?" Zach called out. He and the other ranch hands had seen the lawmen ride in.

"You can let him go," Sheriff Protzel ordered his deputies.

Zach hurried up to the house, and Walker quickly explained.

"You're arresting Walker for Ben's murder?" Zach looked at the lawman, unable to believe what he was hearing.

"That's right. Now, why don't you go get his horse saddled up for him? We need to get back to town."

Zach looked at Walker. He knew with the help of the other hands they could outgun the sheriff and his deputies, but ultimately that kind of a confrontation would only make things worse.

"It's all right," Walker told him, not wanting any trouble.

Zach went out to the stable and returned a short time later leading Walker's horse. He handed the reins over to him. "What do you want us to do, Boss?"

"Let Stacy know what's happened. She's staying in town with Roni."

"I'll get word to her right away," he promised.

Sheriff Protzel and his deputies kept a careful lookout on the ride back to town. They didn't trust Ben's men not to try something, and they were glad when the trip proved uneventful.

It was after midnight when they finally reached the sheriff's office. But despite the lateness of the hour, Mick and the others were still there, waiting out front for them.

And one of them had a rope.

"So, he didn't try to run from you, eh, Sheriff?" Mick said as he and the others closed in around the lawmen as they dismounted.

"Get out of here—all of you." The sheriff drew his gun to make sure the situation didn't get out of control, and he was glad the troublemakers had enough sense to back away. "Walker's my prisoner."

"I like the way that sounds—'prisoner.'" Mick watched as the deputies escorted Walker into the jail.

"Did you hear me, Mick? I said, take your boys and get out of here!" Sheriff Protzel repeated, gun still in hand. He stayed outside on guard, watching them carefully until they moved off. Only when he was certain they were gone did he follow Walker and his deputies inside, closing the door securely behind him.

"What do you want us to do?" Deputy Davis asked.

"Lock him up in back, and then all of you go check around town and keep a lookout for Mick and the others. I don't trust them not to try something tonight."

The deputy took Walker back to a jail cell.

"Make yourself comfortable," he said as he locked him in. "You're going to be here awhile."

He knew the sheriff had his doubts about Walker's guilt, but Deputy Davis had been at the dance and had witnessed Walker's confrontation with Ben firsthand. There was no doubt there had been bad blood between the two of them, and threats had been made.

Chapter Seven

The pounding on her office door roused Roni from a sound sleep, and she got out of bed and quickly threw on some clothes to go answer it. She expected to learn that someone had taken sick or had had an accident.

"I'm Zach, Dr. Reynolds. I'm the foreman out at the Dollar. Is Stacy here?"

"Yes, please come in. I'll get her for you." Roni started back upstairs just as Stacy appeared at the top of the steps.

"Zach's here to see you."

Having already donned her dressing gown, Stacy hurried down to see what the foreman wanted.

"Stacy, I've got bad news." He looked at Roni questioningly, unsure whether to continue in front of the new doc.

"You can trust Roni. What happened?"

"It's Ben Thompson—" he began.

"What about him?" she asked in disgust, wondering what the evil man might have done now.

"He's dead."

"Oh, my God."

Roni was instantly at her side. "What's this got to do with Stacy?"

"Sheriff Protzel and some of his deputies showed up at the ranch and arrested Walker for Ben's murder."

"*What?*" Stacy and Roni were both horrified.

"They brought Walker into town and locked him up," Zach went on.

"I've got to get down to the jail and talk to the sheriff. I've got to get Walker out of there! Wait for me, Zach."

"I'm going with you," Roni insisted.

The two women rushed back upstairs to finish getting dressed. A short time later they were at the jail, pounding on the door.

Considering the volatile situation created by this case, Sheriff Protzel had decided to spend the night at the jail himself rather than leave guard duty to one of his deputies. He unlocked the door to admit Stacy along with the ranch foreman and Dr. Reynolds.

"Sheriff Protzel, you've made a serious mistake," Stacy charged hotly. "My brother didn't kill anybody!"

"Well, Ben Thompson is dead, and everybody at the dance saw the two of them fighting."

"But Ben started that fight!" Stacy insisted.

"Walker is innocent!" Roni spoke up.

"He'll have to prove that at the trial."

"How can you arrest him when you have no evidence against him?"

"I'd say the two of them having a big fight just hours before the murder makes him the prime suspect. Besides, Ben's men are threatening to take the law into their own hands. Walker is safer locked up in my jail than he would be out at the Dollar."

"You're wrong about this, Sheriff Protzel," Stacy told him, growing deadly serious. "You're making a big mistake. I want to see my brother."

The lawman didn't really want to start a battle with her, so he agreed. "You can go on back."

He let the two women into the cell area, then returned to his desk.

Walker had heard the sound of Stacy's voice in the outer office and he was standing up behind the bars as they came in. He was glad to see them, and especially Roni. His gaze met hers as she and Stacy approached.

"Zach—thanks," Walker said to his foreman.

"I got her here as fast as I could."

"Walker, what happened?" Stacy was on the verge of tears, seeing him locked up this way.

"You probably know as much as I do. Evidently, Ben Thompson was killed overnight. The sheriff came out to the ranch and arrested me for the murder. I told Sheriff Protzel I spent the night in my room at the hotel, but he didn't seem to think that mattered."

Roni stepped up. "We know you're innocent."

Walker appreciated her faith in him and her unwavering support. "But everybody else in town is going to believe Mick and the rest of Ben's men."

"Then we'll just have to find the real killer." Roni's mind was already racing as she tried to imagine who would have committed such a horrible crime. Ben Thompson was a hateful man, and she'd known Walker was furious with him. She'd heard him swear to get even with Ben when Jim had been unconscious and they hadn't been certain he would recover, but she knew Walker hadn't meant he was going to sneak off in the night and gun Ben down in cold blood. Walker wasn't that kind of man.

"But how? How will we find them?" Stacy asked, terrified for her brother's safety.

"I don't know, but we will—somehow."

"Talk to Jim. Maybe he'll be able to think of something," Walker suggested, knowing how smart his friend was.

"We're going to get you out of here," Stacy angrily promised, before turning to go out into the main office and talk to the lawman again.

Zach followed her, hoping to help, leaving Roni and Walker alone for a moment.

"I'm sorry," she murmured, moving closer so she could reach out and touch the hand gripping the bars that separated them. She could see the pain revealed in the depths of his gaze.

"I've always known there were people in town who hated me, but I never thought they'd go so far as to frame me for murder."

"Don't worry. You're innocent. There's no evidence that you did it. No one can prove anything. There's no way you can be convicted."

"I hope you're right." Walker met Roni's gaze one last time.

"I'll be back in the morning," she promised.

He nodded as he watched her leave to join Stacy and Zach; then he went to sit on the hard cot. He knew it was going to be a long night.

Roni explained to the sheriff that she needed to return the next day to check on the injuries Walker had suffered when Ben and his men had jumped him after the dance. Then she left the jail with Stacy and Zach. They went back to her house to try to figure out what to do.

"Zach, send one of the boys out to Chet's ranch to let him know what's happened," Stacy directed. "I need him here with me."

"I'll do that first thing in the morning."

"And Walker's going to need a lawyer. I guess Jim can help me with that," Stacy said.

"I wonder how much time we have before the trial?" Roni worried. She knew in Two Guns justice sometimes moved very quickly.

"Jim will know," Stacy said. "We'll ask him what to do."

"Do you want to spend the night here, Zach?" Roni offered.

"No, the men are worried. I have to get back to the Dollar and let them know what's happened."

Zach bid them good night and rode out, leaving Stacy and Roni alone.

They were both too worried to be able to sleep, but they retired to their beds to try to get some rest.

They knew the next few days were going to be hard.

It was just a little after seven the following morning when they left the house to see Jim. Stacy had told him she'd be back to fix his breakfast, and they were pleasantly surprised to find him up and dressed and obviously feeling better.

"Good morning," he greeted them. He let them in with a smile, but as soon as he saw their deeply troubled expressions, he realized something must have happened overnight.

"Jim," Stacy began, "I need your help."

"Of course."

They went to sit in his parlor, and Stacy quickly told him the news of Walker's arrest.

As he listened, Jim was glad he was thinking more clearly this morning and had gotten some of his strength back. He was going to need it. He reached over and took Stacy's hand in his as she poured out her heart to him. He looked deep in her eyes, seeing her pain and fear for her brother's safety, and he knew he had to do everything in his power to help her and Walker.

"We're going to fight this," he promised. "Nothing's going to happen to Walker. The first thing we have to do is hire Ralph Newsome to be his lawyer. We can go over to his office right away. He's a good attorney."

All she could do was nod. Stacy was used to being a strong, independent woman, but Walker's arrest had left her feeling completely lost. She was thankful for Jim's encouragement and support. She just wished Chet would arrive soon. She needed him desperately.

Roni examined Jim and confirmed what he already knew—his condition was much improved.

"I told Sheriff Protzel I'd be over to check on Walker this morning, so I'm going to go there next. Let me know what happens with the lawyer," she told them.

"Tell him I hope we'll have him out of jail today," Stacy said, trying to be optimistic.

Walker's mood was dark as he lay on the hard cot in the jail cell. Though he knew his injuries weren't in any way life-threatening, the pain from his cracked ribs was constant, and he had found it next to impossible to get any rest. It had been a long, painful night.

Walker wanted to get out of jail as fast as he could. Being caged up this way didn't sit well with him. He hoped he could get everything straightened out today and be released. Surely, just the fact that he'd spent the night of the shooting in his room at the hotel would be proof enough of his innocence.

Walker sat up on the side of the cot and stared blindly at the cell bars, thinking about the murder. He found himself wondering, as he had all night long, who'd really killed Ben—and why. A lot of people in the area had had run-ins with Ben, but he couldn't think of anyone who hated the other rancher enough to shoot him down in cold blood that way. He knew it could have been some trigger-happy gunmen just passing through the area, but that made little sense. Ben had been sleeping when the shooting had occurred and no one had made mention of anything being stolen.

The answer was there somewhere, and he had to find it.

Walker heard someone enter the outer office and immediately recognized the sound of Roni's voice.

"Good morning, Deputy. I'm here to check Walker," she told Deputy Davis.

"When he left this morning, Sheriff Protzel told me you'd be coming by," the deputy said. "Will you need to be in the cell with him?"

"Yes, please. I have to change his bandages today." She indicated the bag she was carrying.

"All right. Let's go on back." The lawman got the keys and started over to open the connecting door to the cell area.

"You've got company, Walker," the deputy told him.

As the office door opened, Walker got to his feet.

"Stay back," Davis ordered as he unlocked the cell door to let Roni in.

Walker did as he was told. Roni moved easily into the jail cell and the deputy quickly locked the door behind her.

"Do you want me to stay here with you?"

"We'll be fine," Roni assured him.

"I'll be at the desk if you need anything."

He returned to the outer office, leaving them alone.

"How are you feeling this morning?" Roni asked

as she set her bag on the cot and turned to look him over. She could see the weariness in his expression and knew he'd passed a rough night.

"I've been better," he answered honestly.

"Can you take your shirt off so I can get a look at you?"

Walker unbuttoned his shirt and shrugged out of it as Roni removed a small knife from her bag. She carefully cut away the bandages to examine his injured ribs. Her touch was gentle as she went over his chest and side to check the healing. She looked up at him and noticed that his jaw was tense as she continued to explore his injuries.

"I'm sorry if I'm hurting you," she told him.

"It's all right," he answered tightly.

Although his ribs *were* hurting him, it was her very nearness that was causing the tension within him. He knew this was not the time to be having these thoughts, but the almost-caressing touch of her hands was testing his considerable self-control.

"We're going to need to keep your chest bandaged for at least another week or so."

She moved over to her bag to take out the wrapping and tape she would need to bind him up again.

"Turn your back to me, please," she directed, "and lift your arms."

When he did, her gaze went over the darkly tanned, broad, powerful width of his shoulders in a visual caress. Her attraction to him caused her whole body to grow warm, and Roni scolded herself for her wayward thoughts.

She was there as his doctor, nothing more.

Roni told herself Walker was her patient.

She was determined to be professional.

She reached around him to begin wrapping the bandage tightly about his chest, trying to keep her thoughts on his injuries, not his lean, muscular body. The moment became intimate, though, for she had to move closer to him to adjust the bandage and ended up with her arms around him.

Walker had been controlling his desire for Roni with great effort. Her nearness alone was enough to tempt him, but when she moved against him as she worked with the bandage, he knew he couldn't resist the need to kiss her again. He told himself this wasn't the time or place, but as he glanced toward the outer office and saw no sign of the deputy, his good intentions vanished. Knowing he might not get another chance to kiss Roni for some time, he gave in to his desire for her.

In one easy move, Walker turned in her arms and claimed her in a passionate kiss.

Roni was surprised by his embrace, and delighted. She forgot about the bandage and linked her arms around his neck to return his kiss in full measure. She realized it was dangerous for them to behave this way, but she couldn't resist the temptation. She realized she was taking a desperate chance, but at that moment, all that mattered was glorying in the thrill of their stolen moment together.

A faint, distant sound jarred them apart. They stood there for an instant, staring at each other in wonder, breathlessly caught up in the power of their desire.

Walker made himself turn his back on her again, knowing if he stood there looking down at her any longer, he'd take her back in his arms.

Roni forced her thoughts back to doctoring and quickly set about wrapping the bandage around him.

"There," she said as she made sure it was tight enough to help him heal. "That should hold for another day or two."

He stepped away from her and picked up his shirt to put it back on, knowing putting some distance between them was the safest—and wisest—thing to do.

"Thank you," he told her.

"Stacy's going to speak with the lawyer this morning, so I'm sure you'll be hearing from her soon."

"It can't be soon enough," Walker said, wishing he could walk out of the jail with Roni a free man.

"How's it going back here?" Deputy Davis asked as he appeared in the doorway to check on them.

"I'm finished," Roni told him. She packed up her supplies and the old bandage and stepped over to the door.

Deputy Davis let her out and locked the cell door again behind her.

"Sheriff Protzel said to tell you we appreciate your coming over this way."

"I'm glad to help. If anything changes, let me know."

"We will."

Roni looked back to find Walker's dark-eyed gaze upon her. "I'll speak with you soon."

He didn't respond as the deputy ushered her from the jail.

Alone again, Walker stared around the confines of the cell for a moment and then sat back down on the cot. He could only hope that Stacy would show up soon with good news.

Chapter Eight

Stacy and Jim were just getting ready to leave the house to go speak with the attorney when Chet rode up. The moment Stacy saw him, she rushed from the house and ran straight into his arms.

Jim stood back in the doorway, watching them together. He tried to ignore the jealousy that gnawed at him.

"Oh, Chet, I'm so glad you're finally here!" Stacy began to cry as she hugged her fiancé tightly.

Chet held her close and gave her a quick, reassuring kiss. "I came as soon as I got word."

"Please, come in, Chet," Jim said.

Chet walked into the house past Jim, keeping his arm possessively around Stacy. Jim ushered them into the parlor.

"You're looking a sight better today than you were the last time I saw you," Chet said.

"I'm feeling some better, too. Have a seat," Jim invited, and then he went on to explain all that had happened.

Chet sat close beside Stacy and held her hand tightly to reassure her as he listened.

"What proof do they have that Walker did this?" he asked.

"Nothing—absolutely nothing!" Stacy said in outrage. "They arrested him just because of the fight last night!"

"That's ridiculous. A lot of people had grievances with Ben Thompson," Chet said.

"I know. We were just on our way to speak with Ralph Newsome when you rode up," Jim finished.

"Do you think he'll take the case?" Chet had heard he was a good lawyer.

"He has to! We need the best lawyer we can find," Stacy said fervently.

"Let's go, then. The sooner we get Walker out of jail, the better," Chet agreed, wanting to sound as supportive as he could.

Chet was impressing himself with his own acting ability. He was delighted events were falling into place just the way he'd hoped. Getting through the trial would be tricky, but since there were no other suspects in the murder, he was reasonably certain Walker would be quickly convicted. Then once Walker was out of the way, the Dollar would be all his. Chet silently congratulated himself on his brilliance as he prepared to act the part of the concerned fiancé, eager to take care of Stacy and try to prove his future brother-in-law's innocence.

He hoped his performance was a good one.

* * *

Walker was relieved and hopeful when he heard Stacy and an unknown man talking in the outer office. He went to stand at the cell door, hoping that very shortly Deputy Davis would be releasing him.

"Your sister has hired Mr. Newsome to be your lawyer," the lawman told him as Stacy and the attorney followed him in.

"So am I free to go now?"

"No," Ralph Newsome spoke up. "The sheriff has refused to release you."

"What?" Walker grabbed the cell bars in a rage.

Stacy was standing back in the doorway with Chet, looking every bit as angry as Walker.

"From what I've been able to find out," Newsome explained, "Sheriff Protzel is convinced that Ben Thompson's men are out to get to you, and, honestly, I believe him. There's no way to guarantee your safety if you're released, so he's decided to keep you here until the trial."

"How soon will that be?" Walker demanded, looking at Deputy Davis.

"I don't know," the deputy answered.

Walker's frustration grew. "Look, I didn't kill Ben. Whoever did it is still on the loose! Why isn't someone out there looking for him?"

"Your guilt or innocence is up to the jury to decide." Deputy Davis turned to Ralph Newsome. "I'll be out here in the front office if you need me."

He walked past Stacy and Chet, and closed the door behind him to give them privacy.

Ralph was an elderly, white-haired, stocky man

who'd been in the field of law for many years. He was well-respected in town. He went forward to shake hands with Walker through the bars of the jail cell.

"Jim and Stacy have filled me in on what happened. From the sound of things, it looks like we have a lot of work to do."

"Where is Jim?" Walker asked, struggling to bring his anger under control as he looked at his sister.

"He went back home to rest for a while, then he's going to try to work at the bank a little later today. He's better than he was, but like Roni said, it'll be a few more days before he's anywhere near back to normal."

"I'm glad to know he's at least up and about." Walker turned his attention to the lawyer.

Some time later, after going over all the details of the dance and the two fights, Ralph knew where he had to start.

"Our best and most competent witness is the desk clerk at the hotel. I'll go over there right now and speak with him. He's our main witness as to your whereabouts after you left Dr. Reynolds's office late that night. With his testimony that you spent the night in your room at the hotel, they have no case against you."

"I don't remember speaking to anyone in the hotel lobby at all when I came in, but hopefully the clerk saw me."

Stacy gave Walker an encouraging look as she and Chet left the jail with the lawyer to speak with the desk clerk.

They returned less than an hour later to let him know what they'd found out, and the news wasn't good.

"The clerk says there was no one working the desk late that night, so we have no witness to testify that you went up to your room or that you spent the night there. According to the clerk, you could have come and gone any number of times all night long, and no one would have known. He says he talked to Stacy Sunday morning, and even she didn't know you were in your room."

"But I was—"

"True, you were there then, on Sunday morning, but we have no witness as to where you were during the night."

Walker's anger was growing. He'd accompanied the sheriff peacefully when Protzel had come to the ranch to arrest him because he'd believed the truth would come out and the confusion about his guilt would be easily cleared up. Now, suddenly, things weren't as simple as they'd seemed.

"What are we going to do?" Walker demanded. His feeling of helplessness fed his fury.

"I'll get one of the deputies to ride with me out to where Ben's men found his body," Chet said. "Maybe if we search the site, we'll be able to come up with something that will prove your innocence and get you out of here."

"Thanks, Chet. Right now, from the looks of things, I need all the help I can get," Walker replied.

Playing the part of the concerned future brother-in-law, Chet went out to speak to Deputy Davis and make arrangements for one of the other deputies to go with him. A short time later, Chet and Deputy Warren were riding out of Two Guns.

Ralph stayed on with Stacy to work with Walker and plan his defense. Before they finished, Deputy Davis came in to speak with them.

"I've just gotten word your trial is set for next Wednesday," he informed them.

The lawyer looked more worried than ever. "Thanks, Deputy."

Walker and Stacy looked at Ralph after the lawman had left them alone again.

"Is that good or bad?" Stacy asked.

"It just means we have to work all the harder to get our defense ready," Ralph answered, trying to sound optimistic.

Chet and Deputy Warren covered the long miles toward the location where Ben's men had told Sheriff Protzel they'd found the body.

"It should be up here, not too far ahead," the deputy told Chet.

"Good. The sooner we get there and find something, the sooner I can help get Walker released from jail," Chet said.

"Are you that certain he's innocent?" Deputy Warren asked.

"Yes," he insisted. "If Walker's got trouble with someone, he's not going to ambush them while they're sleeping or jump them from a dark alley, like Ben did the other night."

"How can you be so sure?"

"I know the man."

"But he's a half-breed."

"He may have Comanche blood in his veins, but he's still Paul Stevenson's son." Chet pretended anger at the deputy's remark.

"Yeah, you're right about that." Deputy Warren knew what a fine, honest man Paul Stevenson had been.

They fell silent for the time being as they continued on.

When they reached the general area of the murder, Chet was hard-pressed not to ride straight to the actual location of the campsite. He controlled himself with an effort, taking no risk of giving the deputy any reason to question his actions.

"Keep a lookout for the remains of Ben's campfire. Once we find that, we can spread out on foot and look around," Deputy Warren told him.

It took a while, but the deputy finally found the campsite. They both dismounted and tied up their horses to begin the search.

Chet was concerned for a moment when Deputy Warren found his tracks from the night before. He hadn't realized what a good tracker the lawman was, and he was very relieved when the trail proved impossible to follow over the harsh, rocky terrain.

Though they weren't able to follow the killer's trail, they kept up their search, scouring the area for over half an hour before realizing they weren't going to turn up anything that would affect the case.

"I guess we might as well head on back and tell

Sheriff Protzel we didn't have any luck," the lawman said, taking one last look around.

Chet pretended frustration as he stared off in the distance. "I can't believe we didn't find anything. Whoever killed Ben sure knew what they were doing."

"Yes, it looks like Walker did a real good job."

Chet glared at him. "Walker is innocent."

"Good luck trying to convince a jury of that. We didn't find a single thing up here to help prove his innocence."

"We didn't find anything to convict him, either," Chet countered.

"You sure are sticking up for him," Deputy Warren said in a disgusted tone.

"What about a man being 'innocent until proven guilty'?" Chet pretended anger, but, in truth, he was silently celebrating. His plan was working perfectly. All he had to do was get through the trial. Once that was over and Walker was out of the way, he'd be living on easy street.

Deputy Warren said nothing more as he started over to where he'd left his horse. "You ready to ride?"

Chet said nothing, but mounted up and followed him back to Two Guns.

It was late afternoon when they reached the sheriff's office. Sheriff Protzel was there along with Deputy Davis. Both men looked up expectantly when Chet and Deputy Warren came through the door.

"Did you have any luck?" Sheriff Protzel asked. He'd been hoping for some clue to help Walker's defense.

"No, there was nothing," his deputy told him. "Just a trail that I lost on the rocks, and there's no telling if that had anything to do with Ben's murder or not."

"All right. I'll let Walker know."

"Sheriff—" Chet spoke up.

"What?"

"Do you mind if I tell him?"

"Go on."

He let Chet in to the back area to speak to Walker.

Walker got up and went to stand by the cell door when he saw Chet come in. He was hoping to be freed, but was disappointed again. After Chet told him they'd had no success at the scene of Ben's murder, Walker felt more discouraged than ever.

"I don't know what else we can do," Chet said earnestly. He was more than satisfied to do absolutely nothing from now on except play the role of supportive fiancé to Stacy.

"Talk to Ralph—maybe he'll have some ideas," Walker said.

"I'll do that," Chet promised as he left the jail, hiding his pleasure at the hopelessness of Walker's case.

Chapter Nine

No new leads developed during the days that followed, and as the morning of the trial dawned, Walker found himself even more deeply worried than before. His lawyer had explained to him how quickly a jury could reach a verdict once they'd heard all the testimony, and Walker realized by the end of that day his fate might be known.

Going to stand near the small cell window, he stared out at the sunrise. Memories of his vision quest returned, and he recalled how the spirit had told him of the betrayal and hardship he would face in his life. He understood now what the warning had meant, and he searched his soul for the strength he needed to get through this day and the days to come.

Sheriff Protzel came to the cell with his breakfast a short while later and brought him the set of clean clothes Stacy had dropped off for him the previous day.

"We have to be at the courthouse before nine," he told Walker. "Is there anything else you need?"

Walker looked at the lawman, his expression serious. "Just for the truth to come out."

Protzel nodded in understanding and left him alone to get dressed.

When the time came to leave for the courthouse, Sheriff Protzel warned Walker that all the Thompson ranch hands were in town for the trial. The lawman had expected as much and had arranged for Deputy Davis to accompany them in case of trouble. They took extra care on their way across town and were glad to find that the rowdy men were not waiting for them on the streets.

Nearing the courthouse, they could see a lot of the folks from town milling around outside, waiting for the trial to start, and as they drew near, everyone stopped to watch the accused man pass by. Once they were inside, they started down the narrow aisle in the crowded courthouse. It was then that Walker heard someone call him a murdering savage.

Sheriff Protzel heard the muttered comment, too, and told him in a low voice, "Just keep moving."

Walker showed no emotion and kept moving. He kept his gaze focused on the front of the courtroom. At that moment he spotted Roni sitting with Stacy, Jim and Chet off to the side behind the defense table.

Roni had arranged to meet with her friends earlier that morning, so they could go to the courthouse together. Zach and many of the Dollar ranch hands were there, too, in a show of support. They were all seated directly behind the defense table.

When Roni heard the talking grow louder in the courtroom, she turned in her seat to see Walker coming her way with the two lawmen beside him. Across the distance, their gazes met, and she managed a tight smile, wanting to encourage him.

Walker nodded only slightly in her direction as the sheriff directed him to the chair at the defense table where Ralph was awaiting him.

"Walker," Stacy called his name as he took his seat. She wanted to get up and go to him, to hug him, but knew she had to stay where she was.

Walker wasn't allowed to speak, but he turned to Stacy and gave her a quick, slight smile to reassure her that he was all right.

A few short moments later, the trial began.

"All stand!"

Everyone rose as Judge Richardson entered and called the proceedings to order.

"You may be seated."

"There will be no drinking in my courtroom!" the judge ordered first thing, when he saw that one of the cowboys in the back had a bottle of whiskey in hand. He knew tempers were flaring in town over this murder, and he didn't want any drunks starting trouble in the courtroom during the trial. "Deputy— get that whiskey!"

Deputy Davis went to take the bottle from the drunk.

The judge went on, "And all weapons should have been left at the door. Anybody armed?" He gave a sharp-eyed look around the room and was glad to see that order had been obeyed.

The jury was ready and the trial began.

Luther Evans, the prosecutor, was a thin, dark-haired, sharp-eyed weasel of a man, but he was a smart weasel who used every trick he could to gain convictions. Luther stood up to give his opening statement. "I am here today to find the person responsible for the death of Ben Thompson, and I believe that person is sitting right in this courtroom." He looked over deliberately at Walker. "I intend to prove to you that this man"—he pointed at Walker—"Walker Stevenson, deliberately and cold-bloodedly killed Ben while he was sleeping."

A roar of approval at his accusation went through the courtroom, and the judge had to pound his gavel to restore order.

When the room quieted, Luther Evans went on fervently, "Walker Stevenson had the opportunity to commit this crime. No one saw him during the late-night hours when the murder was committed. Stevenson had ample time to track Ben Thompson down and shoot him. Stevenson also had the motive to kill him. He and Ben had had a fight at the dance. Everyone there saw the fight and heard the threats that were made. I have numerous witnesses prepared to testify to the ugliness of that encounter. I will prove to you that Stevenson hated Ben Thompson with a passion, and hating him as he did, he wanted him dead." He concluded his remarks fervently and returned to sit at his table, looking very smug and confident.

Ralph got up to give his opening remarks. "It is a terrible thing that Ben Thompson was murdered, but my client, Walker Stevenson, had nothing to do with it. Walker Stevenson did not kill Ben, and I am here today to prove to you that he is innocent of the charge against him. Everyone in this room knows what a mean, vengeful man Thompson was. There are any number of folks in the area who had trouble with him, and they could have used this opportunity to frame Walker for the murder. I will prove to you that my client is innocent." He sat back down.

"Call your first witness," Judge Richardson ordered the prosecutor.

Luther called to the stand several witnesses who had been at the dance and had seen the fight and heard the threats. Then he called Stacy to testify.

"Tell us what happened that night," he instructed, after she had been sworn in. "Tell us how Walker attacked Ben Thompson."

"My brother was defending me—" Stacy countered his assertion.

"Don't you mean your *half brother*?" he interrupted snidely.

Stacy fixed a heated glare on him as she responded. "Walker is my brother."

"He is also half Comanche, isn't he? Wasn't his mother a Comanche? He's half savage, isn't he?" Luther taunted her, playing on the jurors' prejudice.

"His Indian blood has nothing to do with Ben Thompson's murder!" she argued.

"Oh, but I think it does," he countered. "Please, go on."

It took Stacy a moment to gather her thoughts before continuing. "Ben started the fight. He hit Chet! Walker fought with him, that's true, but Walker would never shoot anyone in cold blood."

"So you say," Luther replied.

"But—"

"That's all the questions I have," he cut her off.

Ralph got up to cross-examine her, and she repeated her claim that Walker was no murderer. She also testified to seeing him Sunday morning, coming out of his room at the hotel.

Luther called Chet to the stand next. He was sworn in and the questioning began.

"Please tell us what happened the night of the murder," Luther directed.

Chet repeated the testimony of other witnesses and then went on to tell of the late-night encounter near the hotel.

"So there was a second confrontation between Ben Thompson and Walker Stevenson that night?" Luther emphasized.

"Yes. Ben and a bunch of his men jumped Walker and Jim. They'd knocked Jim unconscious and were ganging up on Walker when I happened by."

"And when you saw them fighting, what did you do? Did you go for the sheriff?"

"No, there was no time. I drew my gun and broke up the fight."

"Were any shots fired?"

"Yes, but only after Ben started to go for his gun. I made sure no one was hit. Ben and his men took off after that."

"What happened next?"

"Walker and I took Jim over to Dr. Reynolds's office."

"How angry was Walker after this confrontation?"

"It wasn't a 'confrontation'!" Chet argued, playing his role to the hilt. "It was an ambush!"

"Answer my question," Luther demanded haughtily. "How angry was Walker?"

"He was more worried about Jim than anything . . ." Chet deliberately hedged a little, hoping the prosecutor would sense that Chet was hiding something.

And he did.

"Are you saying he didn't threaten to go after Ben and get even?"

"He only wanted to make sure Jim was going to recover. I didn't stay at the doctor's office for too long. I had to get back to my ranch."

"You're telling this court—and may I remind you that you are under oath—that Walker Stevenson didn't say anything that night about wanting to get even with Ben?"

Chet looked decidedly uncomfortable. "He didn't say anything to me," he answered evasively.

"I didn't ask if he said anything to you." Luther was going after him hard and fast. "I asked if you heard him threaten to go after Ben?"

"Well . . ." Chet glanced toward Walker and saw his strained expression. Stacy, too, was watching him carefully.

"You are under oath," Luther repeated harshly.

"I heard him tell Roni that Ben was going to pay for what he'd done," Chet admitted miserably.

A loud murmur went through the courtroom, and the judge banged his gavel again to restore order.

"Thank you. That will be all."

Chet maintained his serious expression, but he was pleased with the way the prosecutor had dug deep for that information. He certainly hadn't offered it willingly, and Stacy would realize that he'd had no choice but to tell the truth, as bad as it was. When Ralph stood up and began to question him, Chet knew he was going to make it through his part of this trial just fine.

"Chet, how angry would you be if someone had attacked you the way Ben and his men attacked Walker and Jim that night?"

"I'd be furious," he answered quickly.

"And would you say things you didn't mean in the heat of the moment?"

"Yes."

"Do you think Walker tracked Ben Thompson down that night and shot him in cold blood?"

"No. I'm sure Walker didn't kill Ben," he insisted.

"Thank you."

"Next witness, Mr. Prosecuter."

"I'd like to call Dr. Veronica Reynolds to the stand."

Chapter Ten

Roni was sworn in and ready to testify. At first she had expected Luther's questions to be about the extent of Walker's and Jim's injuries from the beating, but after listening to Chet's testimony, she knew he would go after more than that from her.

"Dr. Reynolds, when Walker and Jim were at your office, how seriously were they injured?"

She told him of Walker's cracked ribs, and how Jim had been unconscious for some time before finally coming around.

"And what did Walker have to say about what had happened that night?"

"I don't understand," Roni looked at him.

"It's a very clear question," Luther Evans pointed out coldly. "Please tell the jury what Walker said about Ben Thompson during the time he was there in the office with you. Chet has already told us what he overheard that night. Now, I'm asking you what threats, if any, did Walker make while he was in your company?"

Roni was decidedly uneasy as she faced the prosecutor. "Walker was angry with Ben for ambushing him, and he had every right to be."

"I didn't ask you if he was angry. I asked you what he said regarding Ben Thompson."

Roni looked across the courtroom to where Walker was sitting at the defense table watching her. She wanted to tell the prosecutor that she couldn't remember anything Walker had said.

"Dr. Reynolds, may I remind you, as I reminded Chet, you are under oath?"

"Yes," she answered reluctantly.

"You've said that Walker was angry with Ben Thompson, and rightfully so. What exactly did he say to you? Did he threaten to kill Ben? Did he plan to ambush him and get even? Did he want to see him dead for what he'd done to him and his friend?" the prosecutor demanded, pushing her.

Roni met the man's gaze straight on as she answered him, "Before we knew the extent of Jim's injuries, he said that Ben was going to pay for what he'd done."

Again, a loud murmur went through the courtroom.

"Pay how?"

"I don't know. That's all he said: 'Ben Thompson's going to pay for what he's done.'"

"And just how angry was Walker?"

"How angry would you be if someone had been lying in wait for you and attacked you that way? If Chet hadn't come along when he did, both Walker and Jim might have ended up dead!"

"All the more reason to want revenge on Ben

Thompson, don't you think?" he pointed out. "Why didn't Walker go straight to the sheriff and tell him what happened? Why didn't he want to get the law?"

"I don't know."

"Did he even talk about going for the sheriff that night? Did you?"

"Walker said what had happened between him and Ben was personal," Roni admitted miserably, knowing how condemning her testimony sounded.

Walker knew everything Roni was saying was true, but as he glanced over at the jury and saw how serious their expressions were as they listened to her, he knew her testimony just meant more trouble for him.

"Didn't you think it was strange that he didn't want to see Ben arrested and locked up?"

"I figured it was a situation he would handle by himself."

"And he certainly did 'handle it' himself, didn't he, Dr. Reynolds?" Evans finished with a flourish, not allowing her to say another word. He smiled coldly at her. "That'll be all."

"But—"

Ralph stepped up to question her next.

"Dr. Reynolds, how well do you know the defendant?"

Roni looked over at Walker. He was sitting so stoically at the defense table, and her heart ached. "We've been friends for many years."

"On the night of the murder, how angry was he?"

Roni looked up at the lawyer. "He was very angry because Jim's injuries were so severe. Jim was fortunate that he wasn't hurt more seriously."

"How long did Walker stay at your office?"

"It was late when he left. I'm not certain of the exact time, but it was probably close to midnight."

"Thank you, Dr. Reynolds."

Jim was called upon next. He emphasized his belief in Walker's innocence, but there was little he could add with his testimony.

Mick and the rest of Ben Thompson's men were sitting in the courthouse, looking pleased about the way the Luther Evans was handling the prosecution.

When Luther called Mick to the stand to testify, he eagerly went forward to be sworn in, then sat glaring at Walker from the witness stand.

"I understand you were there when both fights between Walker and Ben occurred. Is that correct, Mr. Jones?"

"Yes."

"Why did Ben Thompson decide to pick the second fight with Walker?"

"He wanted to get even with Walker for humiliating him at the dance, and we were doing a real good job of it until Chet showed up and pulled a gun on us."

"Do you think Mr. Thompson had any intention of killing either Walker or Jim?"

"No," Mick answered.

"How can you be so sure?"

"If the boss had wanted them dead, they'd be dead. He hated the half-breed," Mick said, looking at Walker, "but he just wanted to teach him a lesson that night."

"I have nothing more for this witness. Thank you," Luther said in a satisfied tone.

It was Ralph's turn, and he approached Mick slowly. "Why did your boss like to cause so much trouble in Two Guns?"

"I don't know what you mean," Mick answered arrogantly.

"Well, let me explain it to you. He came into town, got drunk and deliberately started a fight at the big dance. Why would he do that?"

"He didn't start any fight. He just wanted to dance with Stacy," Mick said staunchly.

"There were other available women at the dance. Why did he pick Stacy? She was already dancing with her fiancé."

" 'Cause she's real pretty," Mick said, grinning salaciously at her. "That's why."

"You don't suppose it was because Walker is her brother and Ben knew if he got rough with her, Walker would step in, and he'd have the fight he was after?"

"I don't know," Mick said with a shrug. "We'd been drinking, and we were ready to have some fun."

"And Ben's idea of 'fun' was fighting, wasn't it?" Ralph challenged sharply. "I can call any number of witnesses who've known him over the years who will testify to the fact that Ben Thompson liked nothing better than to cause trouble. It is also a known fact that he hated the Stevenson family, Walker in particular. Isn't that true?"

Mick didn't answer him.

"Isn't that true?" he repeated heatedly.

"Ben had no use for them—any of them. The old man was a greedy son of a bitch who'd do whatever he had to do to make the Dollar the biggest ranch in the area. And Walker—why he's nothing but Stevenson's half-breed bastard!" Mick sneered.

Loud murmuring went through the room.

"If Ben felt that way," Ralph continued, wanting to draw out the complete truth, "then asking Stacy to dance was a deliberate provocation on his part. He wanted that fight, didn't he?"

Mick looked straight at the lawyer. "Yeah."

"What happened after the second fight?" Ralph pressed.

"Me and the boys stayed in town to drink some more. Ben decided to ride on out to the ranch. When we got back the next day and he wasn't there, we went looking for him. That's when we found him—dead at his campsite."

"Were there any clues at the scene to identify the killer?"

"No. There was nothing."

"So, in reality, anyone could have come upon Ben where he was camped out that night and committed this murder, isn't that correct?"

Mick glared at him, his rage showing in his expression. "Walker killed him! Everybody at the dance heard him threaten Ben!"

"Threats are one thing. Murder is another. No further questions."

Mick was cocky as he stepped down. He stared at

Walker as he passed by the defense's table to return to his seat.

Ralph had tried to discourage Walker from testifying, but he insisted on taking the stand in his own defense.

Walker went forward and was sworn in.

Luther approached him. "What time did you go to your room that night?"

"I'm not sure. It was late."

"Did anyone see you enter the hotel?"

"No."

"Did you speak with anyone on your way to the hotel?"

"No."

"Was there a clerk working at the desk?"

"No. There was no one at the desk when I got there."

"So, you have no witnesses who can place you in the hotel at the time of Ben Thompson's murder, is that correct?"

Walker glared at him.

"Is that correct?" Luther repeated for emphasis, wanting to force Walker to answer, zeroing in on what he believed would be the decisive point in obtaining the conviction he wanted.

"Answer the question," the judge directed.

"Yes."

"I'm sorry, I didn't hear you. What did you say?" Luther asked arrogantly.

"Yes," Walker repeated, louder this time, shifting in the chair.

"So there would have been plenty of time for you

to go after Ben Thompson, shoot him and get back to the hotel without anyone knowing about it? Is that correct?"

"I didn't kill Ben Thompson," Walker denied.

"And I say you did. No further questions, Your Honor," the prosecutor said, smiling in satisfaction as he went to sit back down.

Ralph realized they were in trouble. He got up to question Walker, hoping to repair some of the damage that had been done.

Walker watched his attorney walking toward him and hoped his questions could convince the jury of his innocence.

Ralph asked him simple questions to start, beginning with the uneasy relations between the Stevenson family and Thompson, then focusing in on the murder.

"Did you kill Ben Thompson?" Ralph asked Walker pointedly, wanting his answer on the record.

"No, I did not."

"Where did you go after you left Dr. Reynolds's office on the night of the murder?"

"I went straight to the hotel."

"Did you leave the hotel that night for any reason?"

"No. As I told the prosecutor, I was in my room all night. I didn't come out until the following morning."

"Thank you."

It was early afternoon when all the testimony had been given, and the judge turned the case over to the jury. The twelve men went into the small, window-less room to deliberate.

Sheriff Protzel and Deputy Davis took Walker out the back door.

"How long do you think the jury will be out?" Walker asked as they made their way to the jail.

"There's no way of knowing," Sheriff Protzel answered honestly. "I've seen verdicts come in in less than an hour, and I've seen the deliberations go on for several days."

When they came around the side of the court-house, the lawmen saw Mick and two of Thompson's other ranch hands lingering out front.

"Let's cross the street," the sheriff directed.

They had just started to cross when Mick caught sight of them and moved to confront them.

"You'd better keep a good eye on him, Sheriff!" Mick taunted. "I'd hate to have to shoot him for trying to escape!"

"Go on about your business," the lawman ordered.

The troublemakers moved away, but not before giving Walker one last threatening look.

Roni was devastated as she watched the sheriff and his deputy take Walker from the building. The thought that her testimony might ultimately be responsible for convicting him of a crime he hadn't committed tortured her, and knowing there was nothing she could do to change the outcome of the trial only made her feel worse.

"Let's get out of here," Jim said to Roni, taking her arm to usher her through the crowd that was lingering in the courthouse.

Chet and Stacy followed them, glad to be gone from the scene. The trial hadn't been easy on her—Stacy had to struggle to control her emotions. So had Chet, but for completely different reasons. He was delighted with how things had gone, and he believed it wouldn't take the jury long at all to come up with a guilty verdict.

"What do we do now?" Stacy asked nervously.

"It's in the hands of the jury," Jim told her sympathetically. "There's nothing we can do, but wait—and pray." He added the last in a solemn tone.

Stacy looked up at Jim, seeing his inner strength. She realized then what a strong man he really was, and deep in her heart she was grateful for his support.

"There's no proof Walker had anything to do with the shooting. He's innocent," Chet remarked, wanting to try to encourage her. "There's no way they can convict him."

"We know that, but will the jury believe it? The way Luther emphasized Walker's Comanche heritage . . ." Roni worried. "Did you hear the comments some of the people in the courtroom made?"

"I heard them," Stacy said in disgust, "and if the jury feels the way those people do . . ."

They all shared a worried look.

"I need to go down to the bank," Jim told them.

"If you hear that the jury's coming back in, send word."

"I will," Stacy promised. She and Chet accompanied Roni back to her office.

They were going to pass the long, empty hours there, waiting for news of the verdict.

Chapter Eleven

Sheriff Protzel and Deputy Davis settled in the office after locking Walker in his cell.

"Is something bothering you?" the deputy asked, noticing the sheriff's dark mood.

Protzel looked over at Davis and said uneasily, "I got a bad feeling about all this."

"Why?"

"I'm not sure Walker's guilty."

"Who else could it be?" Davis asked.

"Anybody," he countered. "Thompson was nothing but trouble. A lot of folks in the area had run-ins with him, and a lot of folks hated him. But proving it was someone else when Walker had the fight with him at the dance and threatened him right there in front of witnesses—not to mention what happened later . . ." Protzel shook his head slowly. "It doesn't look good for him. No, it doesn't look good at all."

"What else can we do?"

"There's nothing we can do now, but wait."

* * *

Chet sat with Stacy and Roni at Roni's kitchen table.

"It's almost over," Chet said, trying to reassure them. "And once the verdict's in, we can celebrate."

Real soon, now, he knew he'd be celebrating for sure.

"I hope you're right," Stacy said worriedly.

"So do I." Roni was miserable. "I just feel so guilty. The prosecutor twisted everything I said. I know Walker didn't kill Ben Thompson, but Luther made it sound like he'd planned the whole thing."

"Roni, you were under oath, and so was I," he said supportively. "I testified to the same thing. There was nothing else we could do. We had to tell the truth."

"I know, but if he's convicted—"

"Walker knows you had no choice," Stacy said. "But don't even think that way. He's innocent. Surely the jury will realize that."

"How much longer do you think it will take them to reach their verdict?" Roni asked, her emotions on edge.

"There's no way of telling," Chet answered. "We can only wait."

"And, like Jim said, pray," Stacy added.

Walker was sitting on the side of his cot, staring blankly around the jail cell. His mood had grown even darker after returning to the jail. There had been only one other time in his life when he'd felt this unsure of himself and his future, and that had been the day his father had taken him from the Comanche village after his mother's death. It had been hard to ride away from the only life he'd ever known, but somehow he'd made the transition and had adapted to living in the white world.

It hadn't been easy, but he'd survived.

He'd worked side by side with his father to make the Dollar the most successful ranch in the area, and after his father had passed away, he'd dedicated himself to keeping the place running smoothly. He'd wanted to fulfill his father's dream.

And he'd done it—up until now.

Now, Walker knew all that had changed. The things that were happening to him were totally out of his control, and there was nothing he could do to change any of it.

Restless, he got up to pace the cell.

Being helpless didn't sit well with him.

He could only hope that justice would win out in his trial. He had no doubt, though, that some of the people in Two Guns had already convicted him in their minds and were just waiting to see him hang.

Walker drew a ragged breath and struggled for control.

Thoughts of Roni came to him then, memories of the forbidden kiss they'd shared in the cell—the sweetness of her lips, the hunger she aroused in him. He finally accepted the truth of his feelings for her: he loved her. It was a painful acknowledgment, for he feared there could be no future for them.

He was tormented by memories of Chet's and Roni's testimonies and how the prosecutor had manipulated his own words and used them against him. He knew he had no one to blame but himself. His anger at Ben had been real, and Roni and Chet had only told the truth.

In frustration, he sat back down on the cot to bide his time.

He had no choice.

There was nothing else he could do, but wait.

It was less than two hours later when a messenger came running over to the sheriff's office.

"Sheriff Protzel! The verdict is in! The judge said to be back in court in half an hour!"

"Tell him we'll be there."

The sheriff gave his deputy a knowing look before they went back to tell Walker. When verdicts were reached this quickly, he always had a bad feeling about them, and he'd found over the years that he was usually right.

"It's time, Walker," Sheriff Protzel said sympathetically. "The jury's reached a verdict."

Walker said nothing. He got up and stepped out of the cell once the deputy had unlocked and opened the door. As he passed through the doorway, he hoped he would never see the inside of a jail cell again.

They made their way over to the courthouse.

Once the news had gone out that a verdict had been reached, word traveled fast around town. Everyone was hurrying back over to hear what the jury had decided.

Walker had himself under control as he entered the building, accompanied by the sheriff and deputy. He caught sight of Roni sitting near the front with Stacy, Jim and Chet again, and his gaze lingered on her as he made his way to his chair.

Roni sensed the change in the mood in the court-room and looked around to see the lawmen bring-ing Walker down the center aisle. Their gazes met as he passed by, then sat down with his lawyer. He did not look back again, but stared straight ahead as he waited to learn his fate.

He wanted to believe that the jury had recognized the truth and would declare him innocent.

He wanted to believe that very soon he would be walking out of the courthouse a free man.

He wanted to believe the real killer would be found and punished.

He waited.

Roni was tense and on edge as the jury filed in. The moment she'd been dreading was finally upon them. She glanced at Stacy and saw how she was clinging to Chet's hand for strength. She found Jim watching her, and they shared a look of understand-ing as the judge called the court to order.

"Gentlemen of the jury," the judge began, "it is my understanding that you've reached a verdict in this case."

"We have, Your Honor," the jury spokesman an-swered.

"How do you find the defendant, Walker Steven-son?"

"We find the defendant . . ."

A hushed silence fell over the onlookers as they anticipated what he was about to announce.

"Guilty."

A roar echoed through the room.

"I knew he was guilty!"

"The damned half-breed is nothing but an animal!"

"Let's hang him now!"

"No!" Stacy cried aloud.

The verdict slammed into Walker like a violent, physical blow, shattering his self-control. Furious, he surged to his feet, shouting in protest. "You're wrong! I'm innocent! I didn't kill Ben Thompson!"

Roni started to get up to rush to Walker, but she had no chance as the sheriff and his deputy were instantly on him. It took both men to restrain him and force him back down in his chair.

"Order in the court!" the judge exclaimed loudly, banging his gavel forcefully. When things had finally quieted down, he turned his attention to Walker. "Walker Stevenson, you have been found guilty of the murder of Ben Thompson. You are hereby sentenced to life in prison."

"What?" someone yelled in the back.

"He should hang!" another called out.

The judge banged his gavel to restore order again. "There were no witnesses to the murder, so I will not sentence him to hang!"

"But he's guilty!" they were shouting. *"The jury convicted him!"*

"Sheriff Protzel, please make arrangements to have the prisoner transported to the penitentiary. This court is adjourned."

"No, this is wrong! This is all wrong!!" Stacy stood up, crying out to the judge. "My brother's innocent! He didn't do it! I know he didn't do it!"

But no one was listening to her.

Stacy collapsed into Chet's arms as Sheriff Protzel and Deputy Davis made short order of getting Walker out of the courthouse. The way tempers were flaring over his sentence, they feared there might be a riot.

Jim and Roni stood with the others at the front of the courtroom.

"What are we going to do?" Stacy cried.

Roni was heartbroken. "Walker can't go to prison!"

Chet held Stacy close. He tried to sound sorrowful as he told her, "There's nothing we can do now. The verdict's in. It's over."

Jim couldn't believe what he'd just heard Chet say. He glared at him, erupting in his fury at the injustice. "This isn't over—not by a long shot," he declared. "The real killer is out there somewhere, and I'm going to find him—no matter how long it takes!"

Roni and Stacy gazed up at Jim, buoyed up by his determination.

"Thank you, Jim," Roni told him.

"Yes, Jim," Stacy said miserably. "Thank you." He was the only one offering them any hope.

Chet realized he needed to follow Jim's lead. "Whatever I can do to help, Jim, just say the word."

Slowly, they left the courthouse, ignoring the

hateful comments that were being thrown at them
as they passed by.

Two Days Later

The arrangements had been made to transport
Walker to the prison. The trip to the penitentiary
was a long, arduous one, and Sheriff Protzel was
sending Deputy Davis along to guard the prisoner.

Mick Jones and several of the other hands from
the Thompson ranch heard the news and made it a
point to be in town the day Walker was leaving on
the stage. They wanted to be there to give him a
good send-off.

Devastated by the verdict, Stacy had remained in
town, staying with Roni so she could visit Walker
every chance she got. Roni always accompanied her,
and they tried to remain positive when they were
around him. But as the fateful day drew near, Stacy
could no long hide her sorrow from her brother.
They were at the jail that last morning with Jim and
Chet to tell him good-bye.

"Walker, what am I going to do without you?"
Stacy was trying to be strong as she faced her
brother where he stood in the cell.

He was grim as he answered, "Chet and Jim are
here, and so is Roni. Whatever you need, they'll
help you."

She started crying so hard that Chet had to lead
her from the jail, keeping a supportive arm around
her shoulders.

Jim looked at his friend, his expression fiercely

determined. "I'm going to find the real killer. I'm not going to give up until I prove your innocence."

Through the cell bars, the two friends shook hands, then Jim followed Stacy and Chet out to give Walker a last moment alone with Roni.

Roni didn't hesitate. She moved to the cell and touched his hand. Tears filled her eyes as she looked up at him. So many times he had saved her from trouble, and now when he needed her most, there was nothing she could do to help him. Her heart was breaking.

"We'll find a way to free you! Somehow, we'll do it!" she vowed.

He covered her hand with his as he gazed into the depths of her eyes, seeing all her beauty and innocence, and he wondered if he would ever see her again. He longed to take her in his arms and hold her close. He wanted to tell her that he loved her, but the metal bars separating them were a harsh reminder of what the future held for him.

"You'd better go now," he said solemnly.

"But I don't want to leave you. Walker . . . I love you."

The words he'd always longed to hear her say were pure torture for him. "I love you, too, Roni."

"Oh, Walker." She ached to hold him and kiss him and never let him go. "Why did this have to happen?"

"I don't know."

"I'll wait for you. I'll be right here," she promised.

"No, don't wait for me," he told her, wanting her to live her life to the fullest.

Before either one of them could say anything else, Sheriff Protzel and Deputy Davis appeared in the doorway.

"I have to ask you to leave now," the sheriff told her.

Roni nodded and tore herself away, hurrying past the two lawmen to go outside.

Jim saw her come out of the sheriff's office and he went to her. He put a supportive arm around her shoulders and drew her with him to join Stacy and Chet.

The stage would be pulling out shortly and they wanted to be there.

Mick and the others knew it was time. They left the saloon and made their way over to the stage office, eager to see the half-breed off.

Jim was angry as he stood with Roni. "If I thought I could get Walker safely out of town, I'd break him out right now."

"I know. I was thinking the same thing," Roni said, understanding his frustration. "The only problem is, when a wanted man is on the run, folks shoot first and ask questions later."

"Here he comes!" Mick shouted when he saw Deputy Davis leading Walker out of the sheriff's office in handcuffs.

The other men with Mick started hooting and hollering as more folks gathered around to jeer at Walker.

Sheriff Protzel was disgusted by the display, but didn't try to break it up. He didn't want to start a fight. He just wanted to get Walker on the stage without any incidents.

They made short order of getting Walker onboard and then the deputy climbed in after him and closed the door.

The stage driver took up the reins. "You ready?" he called down to the deputy.

"Let's go," Davis answered.

The stage driver hoped the rowdy bunch of cowboys didn't follow them and cause any trouble on the trip. He urged his team on, glad to be leaving Two Guns behind.

Roni and Stacy stood together in heartbroken silence, watching the stage as it pulled away. They caught only one quick glimpse of Walker through the window, and then the stage was gone, leaving only a trail of dust behind.

Chet stayed close by Stacy's side, playing the role of loving, supportive fiancé. He had a lot on his mind. He had big plans for what he wanted to do next, but right then all he could do was bide his time.

Jim was glad the sheriff remained vigilant, standing in the street after the stagecoach had gone. His presence was enough to send Mick and the rest of the crowd that had gathered on their way. Jim nodded his thanks to the sheriff before turning to Stacy.

"Are you going to be all right?" he asked.

"I don't think I'll ever be all right again," she managed brokenly.

"Come on. Let's get you out of here," Chet said. Friend though Jim was to her, Chet didn't want

Stacy getting too dependent on him. She was his. As fast as he could get her to the altar, they were getting married.

Stacy didn't protest. She gave herself into Chet's keeping and let him lead her away.

Roni looked at Jim. "If you find any clues as to who might have killed Ben and you need help, let me know."

"I will. And if you hear anything around town that sounds suspicious—"

"Don't worry. I'm going to be doing all the checking into this I can, and I'll send word to you right away if I find something," she promised. "Is there anything else we can do?"

"Just take care of Stacy. I know that's what Walker wanted." Jim saw the tormented expression on her face. He added gently, "You love him, don't you?"

Roni could only nod and whisper, "Yes."

Chapter Twelve

One Week Later

The sun was beating down and the heat was merciless as Walker stood with the other men in the yard of the penitentiary, dressed in his striped prison clothes with his head shaved. One of the guards walked up to inspect the line of prisoners, while three other heavily armed men stood back, holding the leashes of snarling, barking attack dogs. The guard eyed each prisoner up and down. When he got to Walker, he stopped directly in front of him and smiled coldly.

"Welcome to your new home, *Chief*," he greeted him sarcastically.

Walker knew better than to respond. He waited to see what the guard was going to do next. The trip to the prison had been a long one, and though he'd been there for just a day, he'd already witnessed some of the ugliness that was prison life—the chains and the beatings.

"My name's Taylor. Remember that," the guard told him. "You work hard and do what you're told, and you'll stay alive in here. But don't even think about trying to escape. You see those dogs?"

He pointed to the growling animals.

"They like tearing prisoners apart, don't they, boys?" he asked the other inmates.

They grumbled a "yes" in reply.

"All right, all of you get to work or there will be no meals for you today!" Taylor ordered.

Walker followed the other inmates to the work-site. He'd heard talk that there was the possibility they might be leased out to a chain gang sometime soon, but no one had any idea of when. Walker had come to believe the other prisoners were hoping to be leased out, for life in the prison was as close to hell on earth as you could get. Their beds were bug-infested straw mattresses. There was nowhere to bathe. The food consisted of boiled bacon, molasses, corn bread and coffee. It wasn't much in the way of nourishment, and if anyone dared to say a word in the mess hall, he paid the price. It was a harsh life.

He'd already made up his mind to keep quiet and stay out of trouble.

He knew it was the only way to survive, and he had to survive.

He had to find out who had killed Ben and framed him for the murder—and he had to get back home to Roni.

Thoughts of trying to escape were already entering his mind as he set to work chopping and loading heavy lumber onto the waiting wagons.

* * *

As he finished his whiskey, Chet figured out exactly what he had to do: convince Stacy to push up the wedding and marry him now.

He would play the part of concerned fiancé and try to get her to the altar as quickly as possible. He smiled. He could think of no reason why she wouldn't want to marry him. She'd eagerly accepted his proposal, so moving up the wedding date shouldn't be hard to do. Soon—real soon—the Dollar was going to be all his.

"What are you smiling about, big guy?" Suzie asked as she came strutting up to the bar to stand next to him. She leaned forward enticingly to give him a better view of her bosom, blatantly displayed by the low-cut neckline of her red satin gown.

"Why, I saw you coming and couldn't help myself," he lied to her.

"I'm not used to seeing you in town in the middle of the week. You got something exciting going on?"

"I do now," he said quietly, leering at her with a hungry look in his eyes. He was glad the bar wasn't busy. The fewer people who knew he spent time with Suzie, the better.

She smiled knowingly as she said in a low voice, "I'll meet you around back in ten minutes." She moved away.

And ten minutes later, Chet was there at the back door.

He changed his plan about going straight out to the Dollar. He didn't leave Two Guns until late that night. He decided to pay Stacy a visit the next day.

* * *

It was late when Roni, exhausted both physically and emotionally, returned to her office. She had spent the last, long hours at the bedside of elderly, frail Sarah Mallory. She had given Sarah laudanum to ease her pain, but had known there was nothing more she could do to help her. Sarah's passing hadn't been unexpected. Her family had been with her, but death was never an easy thing to deal with.

After locking the door, Roni went upstairs and got ready for bed. Sleep would not come, though, for thoughts of Walker haunted her. She found herself wondering how he was, and when she would ever see him again. She'd spoken with Jim several days before and had learned that he'd had no luck at all, trying to find a clue to the identity of the real killer. In spite of the discouraging news, she kept alive her hope that they would ultimately find a way to free Walker. Still, she knew tracking down the one responsible would only get more and more difficult as time went by.

Getting out of bed, Roni went to stare out her bedroom window. The moon shone brightly in the starlit night sky. It was beautiful, and serene. She wondered if Walker could see the sky from where he was. She wondered, too, if he was thinking of her.

Her tears began to fall freely as she imagined his suffering, and she knew she'd done the right thing in telling him that she loved him.

Her heart was aching as she turned away from the window to go back to bed.

In the silence of the dark night, she offered up a silent prayer for his safety.

Walker stretched out on the filthy straw mattress and lay there in silence, staring up at the ceiling. He had thought he'd known the meaning of a hard day's work, but today had proved him wrong. Every inch of his body ached, and his hands were blistered and bleeding from the long hours he'd spent chopping wood. Some of the other prisoners had said that being leased out to the chain gangs was even harder, so Walker knew there was nothing to look forward to.

This was his life now.

Turning on his side, he stared out the barred window. He thought of the time he'd spent as a child growing up in the Comanche village and of the freedom he'd known then. He remembered, too, the night of the dance when he and Roni had managed to slip away into the darkness for those few stolen moments alone. Knowing that if he was to survive he must focus all his energy on just staying alive, he fought to regain control of his wayward thoughts. There was no reason to torture himself with memories of the past. He pushed them away, denying them, then closed his eyes and waited for the release of sleep. But even as he fought against it, the memory of those last moments with Roni stayed with him and sustained him.

Chet was in high spirits as he entered the bank to speak with Jim.

Jim had been sitting at his desk in his small office in back when the teller came to let him know Chet was there.

"Send him in," Jim directed. He went to stand in his office door to welcome Chet. "I didn't expect to see you today," he said him as they shook hands. "Come on in and have a seat." Jim closed the door to give them privacy, wondering at the reason for Chet's visit. "Has Stacy heard something new?"

"No, nothing. And I seriously doubt that we will."

Chet took the chair in front of Jim's desk as Jim sat back down.

"I know what you mean," Jim agreed, disheartened. "Then what can I do for you today?"

"Well, I'm here on business," Chet began. "I just heard that with Ben dead, the Thompson ranch is going to be put up for sale. I want to buy it, so I'm going to need a loan."

"All right," Jim said, turning to business. "Do you have cash for a down payment?"

"No, I don't, but I've got my place. I can use that for collateral."

Jim was thoughtful. He knew Chet's ranch was small and, though Chet had made improvements, it was not one of the best in the area. "Do you have anything else you could put up to secure the loan?"

Chet knew what a serious moneyman Jim was, and he had feared the discussion would take this turn. He smiled with easy confidence. "Well, you can count the Dollar as part of it."

Jim glanced at him sharply. "How do you figure that? Your name's not on the deed."

"Stacy and I are as good as married. If I buy up the Thompson place now, with my ranch and the Dollar, we'll really be the biggest and"—he added with emphasis—"*the best* spread around."

"Have you discussed this with Stacy?"

"I wanted to surprise her. As proud as she is of the Dollar, I'm sure she'll like my idea about improving the place even more," Chet declared confidently. He hadn't even talked about it with her yet, but she was going to be his wife, so she would do whatever he told her to do.

"Well, once you have things arranged with her, let me know, and I'll draw up the papers," Jim offered.

"Thanks for your help," Chet said.

He stood up to leave, and they shook hands again. Chet went on his way, but instead of heading to the Dollar to talk with Stacy, he went to the saloon and had a stiff drink at the bar. He'd hoped to pull off the loan without involving her, but Jim wasn't going to let that happen.

Chet knew Jim was a smart man when it came to money. That was why he was as wealthy and successful as he was. It angered Chet that he hadn't been able to convince the banker to go ahead with the loan based on his future marriage. He was going to have to do this all legal-like and convince Stacy to go along with his plan. Stacy didn't know how short on cash he was, and he wasn't about to let her find out before the wedding.

All the more reason to convince her to move up the wedding date. The faster he got her to the altar, the faster he'd get control of the Stevenson money.

Chet threw down the rest of his whiskey and got ready to ride. He had some serious sweet-talking to do that afternoon.

Stacy was in the corral, working some horses, when Zach called out to her that a rider was approaching. She quit what she was doing and left the corral to see who the visitor was. She recognized Chet right away and wondered what had brought him out to the Dollar. She wondered if he'd been in town and heard some news about Walker.

"I was hoping you'd be here," Chet told her as he reined in beside her and quickly dismounted. Uncaring that there were ranch hands nearby, he kissed her and then said in a voice only she could hear, "I was in town for a while, and I've been missing you, so I decided to come by and check on how you're doing."

"Did you hear any news about Walker while you were in town?" she asked.

Rage flared within him at her question, but Chet didn't let it show. Here he'd just ridden all the way to see her, and the only thing she cared about was her brother. "No. I haven't heard a thing."

Stacy looked worried. "I don't know if that's good or bad."

"I would say it's good," he said, wanting to distract her. "If there had been any trouble, they would have sent word."

"Well, I'm glad you're here," she said, finally relaxing enough to smile at him. "How long can you stay?"

"I don't have to be back at the ranch until to-night."

"Good. Come on. Let's go up to the house and visit for a while. I've been missing you, too."

They made their way to the house and, once they'd gone inside, Stacy took a quick look around to make sure Sandy Leeds, the housekeeper, wouldn't walk in on them. When she was certain they were alone, she went back to Chet and kissed him again.

Chet was pleased by her actions. He wrapped his arms around her and held her close as he kissed her deeply. When at last they broke apart, she led the way into the parlor and they sat down on the sofa together.

"So, how have things been going?" he asked.

"Zach and the boys have been a big help. There hasn't been any trouble to speak of."

"That's good. If you ever need me—"

"Oh, I always need you," Stacy said softly.

Chet didn't pass up the chance to kiss her again.

"I love you, Stacy," he told her in a husky voice. "And I wanted to ask you—"

"What?"

"What do you think about moving our wedding up? I know you don't want to elope, but we could talk to the reverend and see if he could marry us in the next week or two."

"Why?"

"Honestly, I worry about you, out here all alone like this. With Walker gone, there's no one to pro-tect you if anything should happen."

His answer surprised her. "You don't have to

worry about me. Zach and the boys are here, and Sandy, too."

"But I do worry about you," he insisted. "And I want us to be together."

"You're so sweet." Stacy sighed, touched by his concern. She leaned closer to kiss him again. "Our wedding day will be here before you know it. You'll see."

"Are you sure you don't want to talk to the reverend?" Chet pressed.

"I'm sure. So much has happened . . ."

"All the more reason to let me take care of you." Chet wanted to slap her, but he hid his anger, tenderly touching her cheek instead. "I want to be here with you every day."

Stacy was completely unaware of Chet's true emotions. She embraced him and sought his lips in a sweet exchange.

Only the sound of the housekeeper coming back into the house forced them to move apart.

"Are you hungry? Would you like some lunch?" Stacy asked. "Sandy should have something ready."

"I'm hungry," he told her as he gave her a wicked, smoldering grin, "but not for food."

Stacy kissed him one last, quick time, and then led the way into the kitchen.

Chet spent the rest of the afternoon with her, playing the role of concerned fiancé, but, in truth, his mood was black. When the time finally came for him to leave, he again took her aside to kiss her.

"Remember what I said," he told her. "Think about it. I want to be with you all the time."

Stacy only nodded and walked outside with him to see him off. She thought it strange that she felt slightly relieved when Chet had finally ridden out of sight. She dismissed the feeling, though, telling herself she was just still upset over all that had happened and needed more time to heal.

Chapter Thirteen

The days seemed endless to Walker. He slaved from sunup to sundown in the blazing heat under the ever-watchful eyes of the guards and their dogs. The other prisoners had heard the guards taunting him about his Indian blood and most of them stayed away from him, wanting nothing to do with a half-breed, and that was fine with Walker. He kept to himself, doing what it took to stay alive, day by day.

The brutality of the guards was never in doubt. If any prisoner showed signs of slowing down in his work, he was beaten viciously. When the guards went after one of the prisoners, the others kept on working, not wanting to risk being punished themselves.

Al Foley was one of the oldest inmates, rumored to be over sixty. He had a reputation for being a hard man. Gray-haired, thin and wiry, he was stronger than many of the younger men and worked harder. Many of the prisoners resented him, for the guards forced them to keep pace with Foley.

It was a brutally hot day. Foley had just finished loading more lumber onto the wagon and had turned away, when one of the prisoners pushed a log toward a guard named O'Malley. O'Malley was standing with his back to the wagon, watching the prisoners work, and had no idea of the danger he was in.

"Look out!" shouted Bryant, another guard.

O'Malley was lucky enough to get out of the way before the log crashed to the ground. Both guards were furious and went after Foley, believing he was responsible.

The other inmates knew better than to interfere. They quickly backed away to watch the old man get what was coming to him. The younger inmate who'd managed to shove the log toward the guard, unnoticed, was enjoying the spectacle as Bryant and O'Malley began to beat him.

Foley was a tough man, but any attack on a guard brought severe punishment. O'Malley and Bryant were out for blood as they pummeled Foley to the ground.

Walker had seen what had really happened and went to Foley's defense. He grabbed one of the guards by the shoulder to pull him off the fallen inmate, but before he could say or do anything more, several more guards who'd seen him make his move joined in.

The prisoners were hooting and hollering in excitement as they watched the bloody battle. More guards came running with their guns drawn to make sure no rioting occurred. The fighting didn't stop until both Foley and Walker were unconscious on the ground.

"What started this?" Parker, the head guard, demanded of O'Malley.

"We were beating Foley, and the Chief jumped in!" O'Malley told him.

"Put the Chief in solitary and use the bat on him when he comes around!" the head guard ordered.

"What do you want us to do with Foley?"

"Leave him there, so the rest of these animals will see what happens if they give us any trouble."

Walker was dragged off to the dark confines of the solitary cell, where he was left chained to the wall.

The pain was excruciating as Walker slowly regained consciousness, and he realized his ribs had been injured even worse. He lifted his head to stare around the dark room and recognized that he'd been taken to the isolated building that was used for prisoners in solitary confinement. The only light coming in was from a small window in the door, just wide enough for the guards to look in. He tried to move, and it was then that he realized the iron cuffs cutting into his wrists were attached by a chain to a ring in the wall. He hadn't meant to make a sound, but he couldn't stop the groan of agony that escaped him as he righted himself and sat up, leaning back against the stone wall to brace himself. The last thing he remembered was trying to help Foley, and he wondered if the other man had survived the beating.

"So, you've finally started stirring," O'Malley' taunted from the door, having heard his groan and the sound of the chains moving.

Walker didn't respond. He just looked up. All he could see were the guard's eyes watching him through the small opening. He had heard the other prisoners talk about what happened in solitary, and he knew he was going to experience that horror firsthand now.

The door opened and O'Malley and Bryant came in.

The sudden harsh light coming through the open door blinded Walker for a moment. When he finally could see again, he realized O'Malley was carrying the weapon known as "the bat." It was a wooden handle with leather straps attached to it that was used for whipping the inmates. He'd seen the scars on some of the other prisoners and knew what was about to happen.

"Turn him around," O'Malley told Bryant.

Bryant started to unfasten the chain at Walker's wrist to reverse his position.

The thought that he was going to be unchained for even a few moments drove Walker to take desperate action. He knew his chances of escaping were slim, but he also knew this was the only opportunity he would have. The two guards had left the door behind them standing open, so if he could get away from these two and lock them in, he had a chance. The solitary building was isolated from the other buildings in the prison, so it was possible that he might be able to find a way out before anyone was alerted to his escape.

When the guard finally released the chain, Walker made his move. He lunged at Bryant, knocking him backward, and then charged O'Malley, who was standing near the door.

Walker didn't get far.

O'Malley was always ready for trouble. He expected the worst from the prisoners and he usually got it. When Walker came at him, he reacted instantly, hitting him savagely. Bryant got back to his feet and rushed to help. The two guards dragged the still-struggling Walker back, stripped off his shirt and chained him up, facing the wall.

"That was a real stupid thing to do, Chief," O'Malley taunted as he prepared to use the bat on him. "I just may have to beat a little more sense into you than I thought."

O'Malley began the punishment, wielding the bat with practiced ease. He enjoyed teaching these prisoners lessons they wouldn't forget. He knew the marks the bat left on his back would remind the Chief for a long time of the mistakes he'd made that day.

Walker locked his jaw against the pain and fought for control as the guard lashed him repeatedly. The pain was agonizing, the leather raising blistering welts upon his back.

"What do you think, Bryant? Think the Chief here has learned his lesson?" O'Malley asked after hitting him five times.

"He deserves a few more—savage that he is," the other guard said, wanting the prisoner to learn his place once and for all.

O'Malley delivered several more violent lashes,

and decided he'd done his job when he finally saw the prisoner lose consciousness.

"That should be a lesson he remembers," O'Malley said as he smiled at Bryant.

"I guess we'll find out when he comes around," the other guard told him. He'd seen some strong-willed prisoners over the years, but this half-breed seemed one of the worst. There was no way of telling whether the beating O'Malley had just given him would break his spirit or not.

They unfastened him from the wall and left him lying facedown on the dirty cell floor, then locked and barred the door on their way out.

It was some time later that Walker finally stirred, opening his eyes to stare around the darkness of the solitary cell. No light shone through the small window in the door, so he knew night had fallen. He tried to shift positions and sit up, but excruciating pain racked him. He stayed where he was, unmoving. Walker told himself he was lucky to be alive after his failed escape attempt, but he wondered what luck had to do with anything right then.

A driving rage sustained him through the long, pain-filled hours of darkness. He knew whoever had killed Ben was still out there. Walker didn't know how he was going to do it, but he became even more determined to escape the hell his life had become and prove his innocence.

He remembered Jim's promise never to give up on the search for the real murderer, and he knew if anyone could find a way to outsmart the killer, it was Jim.

Roni slipped into Walker's thoughts then. The memory of her kiss and declaration of love strengthened his resolve to get through this trial.

In silence, he awaited the coming dawn, trying not to think of what torture the guards had planned for him in the new day.

O'Malley went out to check on the other prisoners as they were bedding down for the night.

"What happened to the Chief?" one of the inmates asked. Many of the prisoners wondered if he'd been killed by the guards.

"Don't go getting excited about the Chief being gone, boys," O'Malley told them sarcastically. "Your friend's alive and well. He's just doing some time in solitary."

Foley heard the exchange and was sickened by it. He'd done his share of time in that hellish place and knew Walker was paying the price for coming to his aid. Foley couldn't remember the last time he'd let himself to be beholden to anyone, but he felt he owed the other man. Once Walker was out of solitary, he would see what he could do for him.

O'Malley threw the door open and stood in the doorway of the solitary cell, staring down at Walker where he sat on the floor.

"Let's go, Chief," he ordered, satisfied that the beating—along with two days of being given no food and only small amounts of water—had taken their toll on the prisoner.

Walker got up slowly and made his way to the door to pass by the guard.

O'Malley smiled when he saw the ugly welts on Walker's back. He knew they would be a reminder to him of the consequences of acting up for quite a while.

"Head over to the mess hall. It's time for lunch," he directed, and he followed Walker there, keeping an eye on him.

When they reached the mess hall, one of the other guards handed Walker a shirt.

Walker said nothing as he started to shrug it on. He gritted his teeth against the pain as he drew it up over his back, then went to sit at his assigned place at one of the tables.

The other prisoners watched him cross the room.

O'Malley went up to the front of the mess hall and looked out across the room. "You boys pay attention to the Chief, here. He just got taught a real good lesson about what happens if a prisoner causes any trouble around here. The same thing will happen to you, if you try anything, so remember that!"

Nothing more was said as the food was dished up.

Having gone without food for two days, Walker quickly downed the boiled bacon and corn bread and drank all the water he could. He wasn't certain if they planned on putting him back to work that afternoon, but he knew he was going to need all the strength he could get.

When the meal was finished, the guards took the prisoners back outside to work. They weren't about to go easy on Walker. They were tempted to put him right back doing hard labor. They knew it might kill him and they didn't really care. Even so, they didn't want to slow the other prisoners down, so they found a different job for him to do for that day.

It was much later that afternoon before Foley got the chance to speak with Walker. He kept it short, not wanting to draw the guards' attention.

"I know what you did that day," Foley told him, "and I appreciate it. Give me some time. I'll make it up to you."

And he did.

When the news came some days later that Walker was among the prisoners who had been leased out to a chain gang, Foley managed to slip him a piece of a file, small enough that it could be hidden on his person. As difficult as it would be, the odds of escaping from the chain gang were better than escaping from the prison.

The day for their departure dawned hot and humid. The sun's glare was harsh as it beat down on the prison grounds where the inmates had been lined up and chained together by the neck. Their hands and ankles had also been chained, for the guards wanted to make sure they had no chance to cause any trouble while they were being transported to the lease camp.

Walker stood unmoving with the other prisoners, watching as the iron prison gates slowly swung open. Waiting there just beyond the gates were the transport wagons that would be taking them away.

"All right, boys. Move it out!" one of the guards shouted.

Chained together as they were, the prisoners had to move slowly through the open iron gates.

"So long—Chief," O'Malley sneered he walked past him.

Walker didn't show any outward response to his taunt. Keeping his gaze downcast, he appeared resigned to his fate, but inwardly his anger raged.

Chapter Fourteen

The prisoners had heard tales of the horrors of working on a chain gang, and they quickly found out everything they'd been told was true. They were kept chained together by the neck for the four days it took to travel to the location of the labor camp. They would be breaking rocks at a quarry situated near a small river.

Once they were in the camp, the neck chains were taken off, but their leg irons remained. Their quarters were flimsy tents with filthy straw mattresses, and the food was worse than what they'd had at the prison. Walker was sharing his tent with a man named Russell, who was in for bank robbery. They had little to say to one another, and that was fine with Walker. He was concentrating on figuring out how he was going to escape. He knew it wasn't going to be easy. Heavily armed guards watched over them constantly, and vicious guard dogs were everywhere. He knew using the river as his escape route was probably his best option, but he was going to have to wait until the time was right.

Each night when Walker was certain the other men were asleep, he took out the file he kept hidden and worked at his ankle chains. It wasn't easy, but he wanted to weaken the chain so that when the opportunity came, he could break them by hand and make a run for it. He was hoping that time would come soon.

It was during the third week in camp that black storm clouds loomed threateningly on the horizon. Lightning could be seen in the distance, and thunder rolled across the land. Though it was late in the day, the guards refused to let the prisoners stop. Even as the storm moved nearer and the wind picked up, they kept the chain gang hard at work.

Walker watched the storm strengthening and knew it was going to be a powerful one. The landscape around them was mostly barren, and he realized they should move to higher ground to avoid a flash flood. But the guards were too intent on getting in a full day's work to worry about any possible flooding. When the storm finally broke, unleashing its fury upon them, the guards raced to get the prisoners back to the campsite.

As they were trying to reach their tents, Walker heard the ominous sound of the rushing water and knew the river was rising fast.

The raging waters were soon upon them, and chaos erupted. The guards frantically tried to move the chained prisoners to safety, but panic set in.

Walker knew the moment he'd been praying for

had come. As the others struggled to get to higher ground, he stopped only long enough to break his ankle chain and then took off running toward the swollen, fast-moving river.

One of the guards saw him make his move, and he yelled to the others to warn them that Walker was trying to escape.

When the other prisoners saw what was happening, they decided to try to make a break for it, too.

Despite the lightning and continuing downpour, the guards were well-trained and quick to react. They unleashed the dogs, turning them loose on the fleeing prisoners. The men gave chase, too, shooting at the escaping convicts as they ran.

Some of the prisoners were brought down, but Walker, unhampered by chains, was too fast. He dodged the bullets and escaped the attack dogs by diving into the gushing waters.

Walker wanted the guards coming after him to believe he'd been shot, so he stayed under as long as he could, swimming with the violent current, trying to put as much distance between himself and the camp as possible. When he finally came up for air, downed tree limbs were being swept along in the current near him, blocking the guards from seeing him. Walker grabbed one of the branches and hung on for dear life as it continued rapidly downstream.

Back near the campsite, two of the prisoners who'd tried to flee were dead and several more lay wounded on the riverbank.

"Did you get Walker?" the head guard demanded as the storm continued to rage around them.

"I hit him," one guard answered quickly. He honestly wasn't sure if he'd shot Walker or not, but he didn't want to anger his boss by admitting that. "I saw him fall. He went under and never came back up."

"You're sure?"

"Yeah, I'm sure, and even if I only winged him, there's no way he could survive being caught up in that flood."

They looked at the river as it tore past them. The storm was showing no sign of letting up, and they knew the flooding would only get worse.

"We'll look for his body when the water goes down," the lead guard said. They got the dogs back on their leashes and started to herd the wounded prisoners back to camp in the continuing downpour. They would come back later for the dead men.

Walker clung to the branch as best he could, but when it crashed into a boulder, he lost his grip. He fought to keep his head above water as he was washed away. It seemed an eternity before he was able to escape the torrent. Struggling with what little strength he had left, Walker finally managed to break free of the river's treacherous hold. In a last desperate effort, he hauled himself out of the water and collapsed on the steep riverbank.

The storm had passed, and darkness was falling when Walker regained consciousness. For a moment, he stared around, trying to remember where he was and how he'd gotten there. His confusion vanished as his memory returned, and he sat up quickly to look around for any sign that the guards were closing in on him. He saw and heard nothing, and the terror that had filled him eased for the time being. If they'd been close, he would have heard the dogs barking. The river was still swollen and running high, and he hoped the fierceness of the storm would convince the guards that he had drowned so they wouldn't search too long for him.

Walker stared at his surroundings, trying to figure how far downstream he'd come. Unsure, he knew he had to get moving. With great effort, he managed to get to his feet and stagger off. As much as he would have liked to believe they wouldn't come after him, he couldn't be complacent. The dogs were trained to hunt the prisoners down, so he had to get as far away as he could, as quickly as possible. The terrain was rugged, and Walker knew traveling on foot would be slow, but he hoped he was far enough from the campsite that he could make good his escape.

Concentrating only on keeping moving, he started west.

He was headed toward Two Guns—and Roni.

He had unfinished business there.

It was near noon the following day when the guards who'd gone looking for Walker returned to the campsite with the tracking dogs.

"Any luck?" the boss asked.

"There was no sign of him. The dogs couldn't find a thing," one guard told him.

"You think there's any chance he lived through that?"

"Not if he took a bullet."

The boss looked uneasily down the river. Knowing Walker was a half-breed, he had no doubt the man knew how to live off the land better than most. A part of him wanted to keep up the hunt, but he realized there was little point.

"All right. Let's get back to work. I'll send word to notify his relatives—if he has any."

The guards thought little more of the lost prisoner. He was a murderer, and they figured the murderer had just got what he deserved.

Two Days Later

"Jim, I need to speak with you. It's important."

Jim looked up from where he was sitting at his office desk to see Frank Carson, the man who ran the telegraph office, standing in the doorway. "Of course, Frank, come in."

Frank entered his office, and Jim could tell he was nervous about something.

"Have a seat," Jim invited.

"No, I won't be staying that long. I just wanted to let you know—"

Standing up, Jim walked around his desk to face the other man. He could tell now that something was seriously wrong. "What is it?"

"A telegram just came in." Frank held it out for him to read.

Jim took the message and stared down at it, first in disbelief and then despair.

His best friend was dead.

"This can't be true."

"Oh, it is," Frank said. "I wired the prison back to make sure I'd gotten the message right, and I did. There's no mistake. Walker Stevenson died in a flash flood at a labor camp." He shifted uneasily. "I know the message was for Stacy, but I thought it would be best to tell you first."

Jim looked up at him. "You did the right thing, Frank. Thank you for bringing this to me. I'll take care of it from here."

Frank said no more. He just nodded and started from the office.

"Oh, and Frank—"

He looked back.

"Don't say anything to anyone else until I've had a chance to speak to Stacy."

"I won't," he promised.

Alone, Jim stood where he was, still staring down at the telegram, wondering what he was going to do. Stacy hadn't yet gotten over the horror of Walker's conviction. Even though she was a strong woman, watching her brother be wrongfully sent to prison had devastated her emotionally.

And now this.

He thought of Roni and knew the news would be heartbreaking for her, too.

Miserably, he sat back down at his desk, the telegram still held tightly in his hand. The knowledge that Walker was dead tore at him. His weeks of searching for a lead in the murder had turned up nothing, and the injustice of it all filled him with rage.

It took Jim some time before he was able to leave the privacy of his office and go to Stacy. No matter how he told her, he knew this was going to be the most difficult thing he'd ever done.

The ride he made to the Dollar was the longest of his life.

Stacy was up at the house when she heard the ranch hands call out that someone was riding in. She went out the front door to see who was coming and was surprised to find it was Jim. Though she was always glad to see him, having him show up this way in the middle of the day left her concerned about the reason for his visit.

Jim had been dreading this moment ever since he'd gotten the news in town, and seeing her standing there, looking so beautiful and innocent as she watched him ride in, just made it that much harder. He was about to completely shatter her world, yet there was nothing else he could do.

"I didn't expect to see you today," Stacy greeted him as he reined in and dismounted.

"Stacy," Jim began after he'd tied up his horse and turned to her. "A telegram came today—"

Stacy tensed and her eyes widened as she stared at the piece of paper he was holding in his hand. "What is it?"

"We'd better go inside," he said quietly.

She glanced up at him quickly and then hurried

back into the house. She spun around to confront him as he came through the door. "Is it about Walker? Is he all right?"

"It's from the prison authorities," he began painfully.

"Why are they sending me a telegram?" Stacy demanded.

"According to them, Walker was on a chain gang that got caught up in a flash flood and—"

"*No*," she protested, fear filling her heart.

"Stacy—"

"*No!*" She didn't want to hear what she knew was coming. She started to back away from him.

Jim saw the panic that gripped her and quickly moved to take her in his arms. "I'm sorry, Stacy. I'm so sorry. Walker drowned—"

Stacy was sobbing, and she fought against Jim's hold for a moment, pounding on his chest with her fists, trying to make it all go away, and then suddenly she collapsed against him, weeping inconsolably.

Jim didn't hesitate. He lifted her in his arms and carried her into the parlor. Sitting down on the sofa, he cradled her to him, wanting to absorb her pain, wanting somehow to make things better for her, and yet knowing no matter what he did, he couldn't change what had happened.

They remained that way for a time, caught up in the nightmare of their loss.

Stacy finally drew a shaky breath and tried to steady her runaway emotions. She had always considered herself a fairly strong woman, but the sorrow that had come into her life lately was too much for her to bear alone. She was immensely grateful for Jim's comforting presence.

"Are you all right?" Jim asked in a gentle voice as her crying quieted.

Stacy lifted her head to look up at him. "I don't think I'll ever be all right again."

"I know," he said as he drew her head down to his shoulder and kissed her softly on the forehead. "I know."

Zach's unexpected call at the front door forced Stacy to try to pull herself together.

"Stacy, is everything all right?" He had been working out at the stable when he'd seen Jim ride in and had wondered at the reason for his visit.

"Zach—"

He frowned when he heard her choked voice, and when she came to the door to let him in, he could tell by her tear-ravaged face that something was terribly wrong. He entered the house as Jim came to join them.

"What is it? Is there anything I can do?" He looked between them.

"There's nothing anyone can do," Stacy managed. "Walker's dead."

Zach was shocked, and he listened in horror as she told him what little they knew.

"I'm sorry, Stacy." His words were heartfelt, for he had the greatest respect for Walker. They had been friends.

She looked up at him. "Will you tell the men for me?"

He nodded. "If you need anything—"

"Could you send someone to let Chet know, too?"

"Right away."

When Zach had left them, Jim looked down at Stacy. She seemed so fragile he wanted to continue holding her, but he held himself back.

"Did you tell Roni?" Stacy asked him.

"No. I came straight to you."

"She has to know. We have to go to her."

"I can tell her when I get back to town," Jim offered.

"She'll need both of us there."

He nodded in understanding.

Chapter Fifteen

*E*mily, push! Push as hard as you can!" Roni urged Emily Stafford, as the young women struggled to give birth.

Roni knew Emily's pregnancy had been a difficult one and now she'd gone into labor a month earlier than expected. Emily had been having contractions for hours now, and Roni feared the baby might not survive. She was worried about the mother's condition, too.

Emily let out a tortured scream, growing weaker by the minute, and Roni knew she had to do something to help.

"I'm going to use the forceps," Roni told her.

Emily was too shaken even to answer as Roni carefully set to work.

Out in the hallway, George Stafford paced anxiously up and down in front of the closed bedroom door. His wife's agonized screams tore at him, leaving him feeling helpless and frustrated. He'd started into the room several times, but stopped each time, knowing Dr. Reynolds was there and he would only be in the way.

When a loud, hysterical scream erupted from the bedroom, George stopped in his tracks and went pale. He stood there, staring at the door, waiting—praying—

It seemed an eternity passed before the bedroom door slowly opened.

Roni found George anxiously standing there and she quickly put his fears to rest with a smile. "I think you should come in and see your son, George."

"Emily—?" He looked questioningly past her into the room.

"She's going to be all right and so is your baby."

"Really?"

"Really," she assured him. "Go on—They're waiting for you."

"Thanks, Doc—" George rushed into the bedroom to see his wife and newborn child.

Roni was in a good mood when she returned to her office. The delivery had been difficult, but the baby and his mother were both doing well. Childbirth was never easy or simple, but seeing the newborn in his mother's arms was wonderful.

Roni had just started to settle in when she heard a knock at the door. She went to answer it and found Stacy and Jim there.

"Roni, we need to talk to you," Jim said.

"Of course, come in." She knew immediately something serious had happened, just by the tone of his voice, and she held the door wide for her friends to enter.

When she'd closed the door behind them, they faced her.

"Roni, there's been some bad news," he began.

Roni looked at Stacy and terror seized her heart when Stacy lost control and began to cry.

"What is it?" Roni asked as Jim put an arm around Stacy.

"It's Walker—" he began.

"Oh, Roni, Walker's dead—" Stacy choked out as she clung to Jim for strength.

"Dead? He's dead?" she repeated, stunned. "No, that can't be. It's got to be a mistake!"

Stacy went to Roni and put her arms around her, offering her what support she could, while Jim explained what they knew.

"But do they know for sure he drowned?" Roni challenged.

"According to the telegram—yes," he answered.

"Did they find his body?"

"Well, no, but—"

"Then Walker could have escaped. He could have gotten away—"

"He was on a chain gang at a lease camp," Jim said, taking out the telegram and showing her the message.

"This can't be," Roni stared down at it in disbelief. The thought of what Walker had suffered, caught up in a flash flood while he was in chains, sickened and horrified her. "Oh, Jim—Stacy—"

The two women clung tightly to each other as they grieved.

"I loved him so," Roni wept.

"I know."

"We all did," Jim added solemnly.

Roni went to Jim and hugged him, knowing he'd lost his best friend.

When the initial shock had worn off, they went upstairs to sit in Roni's parlor.

Roni was emotionally numb. "I always believed we'd find the real killer. I always believed Walker would be proven innocent and come back—"

"So did I," Jim said fiercely. "And I'm not going to quit looking for the man who killed Ben. He's the one responsible for all of this."

"We're still going to clear Walker's name," Roni swore.

"Thank you," Stacy said with heartfelt emotion.

They stayed together for a while longer, trying to understand how this tragedy could have happened, but they could find no answers.

"Do you want to spend the night here, Stacy?" Roni invited, knowing how lonely she would be back at the ranch.

"No, I have to get back. I had Zach send word to Chet, but I haven't had the chance to see him yet. He may be at the Dollar waiting for me."

"If there's anything you need—if there's anything I can do, just let me know," Roni offered.

"I don't think there's anything any of us can do now," Stacy said sadly.

Roni saw them out, and then went back upstairs to her bedroom. Her heart was aching as she gave in to her tears. She only wished she had had more time with Walker, time she could have spent showing him how much he meant to her. She sat down weakly on the side of her bed. A part of her wanted to believe it was all a lie, that Walker was alive and on his way back to her. Roni told herself it was wrong to give herself false hope, but she couldn't accept that Walker was lost to her forever. Lifting her gaze to stare out the window at the sun, low in the western sky, she wondered how she would go on.

Injured and exhausted, Walker forced himself to keep moving across the harsh terrain. It would be sundown soon, and he had to find shelter before darkness claimed the land. His ankles were bloodied from the metal cuffs he still wore, but the pain didn't stop him. When he came across a small watering hole, he made camp there.

His years among the Comanche had taught him how to live off the land, and he called upon those long-ago lessons now to survive. He found persimmons and dug up some Indian potatoes and wild onions to eat raw. He wanted to build a fire, but feared the guards were still tracking him. The desolation and loneliness of the night brought back memories of his vision quest. As he sought what comfort he could find on the hard ground, he remembered the warnings the spirit had given him about betrayal and hardship in his life, as well as the promise of love and friendship.

Walker knew he had found love with Roni, but the thought of the betrayal haunted him. He found himself wondering if someone close had set him up for the murder. He tried to figure out who would benefit from his arrest and conviction, but the only person who stood to gain anything from it was Stacy. With him out of the way, the Dollar would be all hers, but he knew his sister well enough to be certain she would never betray him.

There were people in town who disliked him, but none of them had anything to gain by framing him for murder. He thought of the hands at the ranch and wondered if any of them held a grudge against him, but he had had no run-ins with any of the men working for him. They had all seemed loyal and hardworking.

Walker thought of Chet then and frowned. Chet was the only other person who would benefit from getting rid of him. The Dollar would be Chet's once the rancher married Stacy, but even as Walker considered the possibility, he knew the idea was ridiculous.

Chet was the one who had rescued him and Jim from Ben and his men that night in the alley.

Chet was his friend.

Still unable to find an answer, Walker sought rest. At least in sleep, he would find peace—for a little while.

Chet had been out working stock and didn't get back to his ranch house until late. One of his hands had been watching for him and quickly went to speak with him.

"Zach, the foreman from the Dollar, rode in today.

He left a note for you up at the house. He said to make sure you got it as soon as you returned."

"Did he say what it was about?" Chet was surprised. The last time anyone had ridden over from the Dollar had been the day Walker had been arrested.

"No."

Curious, he left his horse at the stable and went up to the house. He found the note on the kitchen table and quickly read it.

Chet— Jim brought word today that Walker has been killed in a flash flood. Stacy's gone into town with him to tell Roni.

Chet stared at the message long and hard, first with disbelief and then with a great sense of satisfaction. He couldn't believe how well things were working out for him. He couldn't have planned it any better if he'd tried.

Chet went to the cabinet where he kept his liquor and poured himself a glass of whiskey to celebrate. As he sat down at the table to enjoy his drink, he wondered whether he should ride for the Dollar that night or wait until daylight. He wasn't sure whether Stacy would make it back to the ranch tonight or end up spending the night in town. The last thing he wanted to do was listen to her sobbing and mourning about her dead half-breed brother, but he knew he had to play his role to the best of his abilities—until they were married.

With that final thought, Chet finished off the whiskey and went to get cleaned up. He would head out to see Stacy. The worst that could happen would be she wouldn't show up until the following day, and that was all right with him.

Jim and Stacy said little on their ride back to the ranch. Jim drove the buggy at a slow pace, wanting to spend as much time with Stacy as he could. She had been there for him when he'd been injured; he could do no less for her. As they drew close to the Dollar, he looked over at her and saw how she was struggling for control.

Stacy felt his gaze upon her and looked back at him. "Do you think Roni could be right? Do you think Walker is still alive out there somewhere?"

Jim understood her need to cling to what little hope they could find, but he also knew it would be cruel to give her hope when there was none.

"There's nothing I'd like more than to hear this was all a mistake, but the officials wouldn't have sent the telegram if they'd thought Walker had gotten away and was still on the loose. They would have gone after him and tracked him down. Prisoners don't escape from a chain gang."

Stacy had heard the horrible tales of what life was like in the convict lease system, and she understood why Jim was being so honest with her.

Reaching out, Jim took Stacy's hand in his in a supportive gesture. Her hand was small and felt delicate to him, and he realized just how fragile she really was. The love he felt for her caused his heart to constrict. A surge of protectiveness filled him, and he knew he would do whatever was necessary to help her through this hard time and keep her safe.

Stacy held his hand tightly, needing his strength.

It was almost dark when they drove up to the house. A few of the hands were still out by the stable and they waved as they passed by. Jim was expecting to find Chet, watching and waiting there for Stacy. He was surprised and, he had to admit, glad when they discovered the house was dark. Relieved that Chet wasn't there, he reined in and got out to help Stacy from the buggy.

Gentleman that he was, it was an innocent gesture on his part. He put his hands at her waist to lift her down, and she rested her hands on his shoulders to steady herself. But as he lowered her to the ground their gazes met, and, for that instant, as her body brushed against his, it was just the two of them, alone in the world.

Stacy gazed up at him. She had always thought Jim was good-looking, but in the shadows of the fading twilight, he looked even more handsome. She saw his inner strength and his gentleness. She saw his pain, and she saw something else in his eyes that left her momentarily breathless.

Jim was gazing down at Stacy, intensely aware of her nearness. He wanted to keep her in his arms forever, but he forced himself to release her and step back, distancing himself from the temptation she presented.

"Will you come in for a while?" she asked, feeling so very alone now that he'd moved away from her.

"Just for a minute," he answered.

He followed her inside and stood back, watching her as she went to light the lamp in the parlor.

"Are you all right?" He was concerned about leaving her by herself this way.

Stacy was honest as she came back to stand before him. "I don't know," she said wearily.

Jim couldn't help himself. Ever so carefully, he took her in his arms. It was meant to be a supportive embrace, to encourage her and help her be strong in her loss. The moment he held her close, though, she sighed his name, and he lost the last remnant of his self-control. Tenderly, he bent to her and claimed her lips in a gentle caress.

Stacy held herself stiffly for a moment. She told herself she was engaged to Chet. She told herself it was wrong to be in Jim's arms this way, but as his lips moved persuasively over hers, she gave herself over to his embrace. She lost herself in the thrill of his kiss.

It was heavenly torture for Jim to be holding Stacy and kissing her, and when he felt her response, it was that much more painful for him to end the kiss and reluctantly put her from him. He gazed down at her, seeing her flushed cheeks and the look of confusion in her eyes.

"Stacy, I'm sorry. That should never have happened," he apologized.

Stacy just stood there for a moment, staring up at him. She was stunned by her own reaction to his kiss, and by the way he had ended it so suddenly and was now regretting that he'd done it.

When she didn't respond, Jim figured she was upset with him and quickly excused himself, turning to leave. "I'd better go."

"Jim, wait." Stacy started to go to him but just then she heard someone ride up in front of the house. She glanced out the window to see Chet reining in by the buggy.

Jim heard him, too, and knew it was definitely time to leave. Stacy's kiss had been as wonderful as he'd always imagined it would be, but she was engaged to Chet.

"It looks like Chet's here," he offered. "I'll be in touch."

Jim hurried outside, and Stacy followed him. They found that Chet had already dismounted and was heading inside.

"I came just as soon as I got the message," he told them. He quickly went to Stacy and put an arm around her to draw her close to his side. "Is it true? Is Walker—"

Stacy nodded, unable to speak.

Jim answered for her. "The telegram arrived earlier today, and I brought it to Stacy as fast as I could."

"I appreciate your help, Jim," Chet said.

For some reason, his statement irritated Jim, but Jim didn't let his reaction show. He looked at Stacy and then back at Chet. "Take care of her."

"I will."

Seeing Stacy standing so close beside Chet troubled him, and he knew he had to leave before he did something rash. "I have to go."

"Jim—" Stacy felt even more devastated now that

he was going. She left Chet's side and went to Jim, touching his arm. "Walker was blessed to have a friend like you—and so am I."

Jim covered her hand with his and gave a slight nod. With a quick glance at Chet, he turned away and strode off to the stable where he'd left his horse earlier in the day.

Chet had to admit he was glad to see Jim go. There was something about the way Jim and Stacy were acting that bothered him, something about the way they'd looked at each other. He frowned slightly. True, Jim had been the one to give Stacy the bad news and help her through the shock of it. He was glad about that, for it had taken a load off him not to have to worry about all her weeping and misery. It was going to be hard enough for him to keep up the pretense of mourning for these next few weeks, but he would do it. In the meantime, now that Stacy truly was alone and obviously in need of his protection, he grew even more determined to move up the wedding.

"Let's go inside," Chet said, guiding her to the door.

Stacy cast one last glance in the direction Jim had gone and then let Chet take her back into the house. They settled in the parlor to talk for a while. Chet wisely didn't bring up the subject of their marriage. He just played the role of the concerned fiancé, intent on helping her in any way he could.

"We're going to make it through this," he reassured her as he held her close beside him on the sofa.

She only nodded.

Chet decided to try to distract her, and he bent to kiss her.

Stacy accepted his embrace, but felt nothing.

It irritated Chet that she didn't really respond to him, but he controlled his anger as he broke off the kiss.

"You look tired," he told her.

"It has been a long day," she admitted, shifting a little away from him on the sofa. She knew he was trying to be considerate of her, but she found little solace in his nearness.

"Why don't you go on to bed?"

"I think I will. Are you going to stay the night?"

"Yes. I'll bed down out at the bunkhouse." He would rather have stayed in the house and shared her bed, but he knew this wasn't the time. He gave her one last gentle kiss and then got up to leave. "I'll see you in the morning."

She walked with him to the door.

"Good night."

When Chet had gone, Stacy went to her room and got ready for bed. She was drained, physically and emotionally, as she stretched out on the bed's welcoming softness. She expected to fall asleep right away, but sleep eluded her. The memory of Jim's embrace stayed with her. She had always liked and admired Jim. He was a kind man and a very smart one, but until tonight, during that one breathless moment when he'd taken her in his arms and kissed her, she'd never thought of him in any way other than as a friend, but now . . . The heat of his

kiss and her own response to it had startled and un-
settled her, especially when she compared it to kissing Chet good night.

Stacy realized she should have felt those passionate emotions in Chet's embrace.

Chet was her fiancé.

They were to be married.

The thought haunted her as she stared off into the
darkness. She felt empty emotionally, and alone—
so very alone.

Chapter Sixteen

$\mathcal{M}$ile after mile, Walker kept heading toward home. He lived off the land, eating what fruits and plants he could find. After the sixth day out with no sign of the guards or their dogs coming after him, he decided it would be safe to build a small fire when he made camp.

Walker found a secluded spot near some mesquite trees to bed down for the night and was gathering up sticks, stones and dry grass to make the fire, when a rattlesnake struck at him. He managed to avoid its fangs and killed the snake with a rock. He had always understood the importance of having his knife with him, and he missed it now more than ever.

Walker hadn't eaten rattlesnake since his childhood in the village, but hungry as he was, he knew he had his dinner. He took the snake back to the campsite, and using a sharp-edged rock, he prepared it to cook over the small fire he built. Once it was roasted, he ate it quickly. He thought of the food he'd been given at the prison and knew the snake tasted better.

Walker picked up the sharp-edged rock and stared down at it. It was as close to a knife as he was going to get right now, so he decided to keep it with him.

The memory of using his knife to save Jim's dog came to him then. Though he had been thrown out of school for his action, that was the day their friendship had been sealed. That had also been the day he'd come to know Roni. He smiled, his first in many days.

At dawn, he moved out again.

It was late the next afternoon when he topped a low rise and saw a small ranch in the valley below. Staying out of sight, he kept watch to see how many people were around. He knew there would be little sympathy for him as an escaped convict, so he had to be careful. He was surprised to find that there didn't seem to be anyone in the house. He waited until dark, knowing the rancher might be out working stock, but when no one returned, he carefully made his way down to the house.

Staying low, he crept up and looked in a window to find there was no one inside. He went out to the stable next and checked inside it, too. There were several horses in the corral, and he took care not to disturb them. He didn't want the animals to alert anyone to his presence. Walker's relief was great when he found the stable deserted.

He knew he had to take advantage of the situation and work fast—real fast. He found a lamp and some matches inside and quickly lit the lamp, so he could see what he was doing. He searched for the tools he needed to remove the iron cuffs. He found them and went to work. It took a while to break them off, but he finally did it. His ankles were bloody and sore, but he was completely free, at last.

Walker took the cuffs with him as he went up to the house. He left the irons on the small porch and went inside. It was obvious the folks who lived there hadn't been gone very long, probably on a trip to the nearest town. The place was clean, and there was some food in the pantry. He wasted no time fixing himself a plate of beans and beef jerky. He devoured it quickly, then set about looking for clothes. He found a pair of men's pants and a shirt that would fit and quickly went outside to wash up and change. He considered spending the night there, but knew it was best that he keep moving.

Going back into the house, Walker took some more beef jerky, and though he found no guns, he did take a knife to carry with him. Taking up a pen, ink and a piece of paper, he left the owners a note thanking them and promising to return the horse he was borrowing and to repay them for what he'd taken. He did not sign his name. He would identify himself to them later when he returned to repay their hospitality.

It was near midnight when he rode away. He took the irons with him, not wanting to leave behind any clues to his whereabouts.

Stacy tried to go back to her normal routine. She thought if she kept busy, she wouldn't think about

Walker so much. Being the sole owner of the ranch was a big responsibility, and demanded a great deal of her time and energy. She owed it to Walker and her parents to keep the Dollar successful.

Chet was being attentive, making regular visits. She appreciated his company, but she had to admit that she hadn't been able to forget Jim's kiss. She hadn't seen Jim since that day, and she found she missed him. Chet was coming to dinner that night, so she quit working early to get cleaned up and help Sandy with the cooking.

Sandy was the wife of one of the hands, and as much as Stacy had always appreciated her hard work, now that she was running the Dollar alone she appreciated the housekeeper's help more than ever.

Chet showed up right on time. He had a lot on his mind, and he knew he had to work on convincing Stacy to move up the wedding date.

"You look real pretty tonight," he said, eyeing her as he followed her into the house.

"Why, thank you," Stacy replied with a smile.

Once they were inside, he asked, "Is your cook still here?"

"No, she's gone for the day."

Knowing they were alone, Chet wasted no time taking Stacy in his arms and giving her a kiss.

She was a little surprised by his ardor, but she linked her arms around his neck and returned the kiss.

"I've been missing you," he told her, "and I've been worrying about you."

"There's no need to worry."

"But I do." He looked down at her, keeping his expression filled with tenderness and concern.

"You're sweet," Stacy said, lifting one hand to touch his cheek.

"No, you are," he replied, kissing her one more time.

They went into the kitchen, and Stacy served up the dinner she and Sandy had prepared. They had fried chicken, fresh rolls and greens, along with Sandy's apple pie for dessert.

"That was delicious," Chet complimented her as he finished off his piece of pie.

"I'm glad you enjoyed it."

"It won't be too long before we'll be having supper like this every night."

Stacy just smiled at him.

He went on, "I've been thinking, once we're married, the two of us are going to have the biggest and the best spread in the area. I heard some talk that the Thompson ranch might be going up for sale soon, and if it does, we ought to buy it."

She was put off by the idea. "There's no need to buy the Thompson place. I've got enough to handle just running the Dollar."

"I'll be running things once we're married," he said arrogantly.

Stacy wanted to remind him that they weren't married yet, but she held her tongue. She was still dealing with the horror of Walker's death and was in no mood for an argument. "Chet, I'm just not ready to start thinking about all that yet."

He looked at her, his expression sympathetic. "That's why, when Walker first left, I thought we should move up the wedding date. I knew this was going to be too great a responsibility for you to handle all by yourself after all you've been through."

Stacy couldn't believe what she was hearing. She couldn't believe Chet thought she was incapable of managing the Dollar. Her father and Walker had taught her everything she needed to know to run the ranch, and she intended to do just that.

Chet went on, unaware of her inner reaction. "Maybe now you'll decide to change your mind about the wedding. You know I love you, and I just want you to be safe and happy. If we got married now, I'd be here to help you all the time. I hate that you're here alone."

Tears welled up in her eyes at his words, and she realized he had no idea how being reminded that Walker was never coming back tore at her heart. "No. I'm not ready—not yet—"

He nodded as if he understood her misery, but in truth he wanted to throttle her for being so stubborn and bull-headed. "When I was in town last, there were rumors going around that the railroad might be coming through soon. If it does, we could stand to make a lot of money."

She could hear the eagerness in his voice as he thought about being so rich, but money was the last thing on her mind. "Oh, Chet, I just can't think about all that right now. There's just too much happening—too much going on."

"I understand. I only want you to know things are looking up for us."

"I know things will eventually get better, but right now, it's so hard."

Chet couldn't believe she cared so much about her brother. He got up and went to her, drawing her out of her chair to hug her. He kissed her sweetly. "I'll always be here for you. You know that."

"I know."

Stacy accepted his kiss, but felt no desire. They talked for a little while longer, and once again, she found she was relieved when he finally rode away. She went to the kitchen to start cleaning up.

Sandy had seen Chet leave and she came to help with the kitchen chores.

The housekeeper took in Stacy's troubled look and asked worriedly, "Is everything all right?"

Stacy didn't realize she was being so obvious about her confused feelings for Chet, and she quickly masked her emotions. "I'm fine. Just tired, I guess."

"You have had a long day. Go on to bed. I'll finish things up here."

"Are you sure?"

"Yes. Go on."

Stacy didn't need any further encouragement. She retired to her bedroom and quickly went to bed. She couldn't help wondering, though, what Jim was doing right then.

In Two Guns, Jim was having a drink at the Ace High—alone. He wasn't really much of a drinking man, but his mood had been so dark lately, he'd decided he needed some distraction.

Antonio, the bartender, was glad to see him. Everyone in town knew how wealthy the banker was, so Antonio figured Jim would be spending some money tonight.

When the saloon girls saw Jim come in, they made bets among themselves to see who could work her magic on him and get him upstairs the quickest. They were eager to help him part with his money; besides, he was a far cry better looking than the usual clientele they had to deal with.

"How's it going?" Antonio asked, just to make conversation as he poured Jim a tumbler of whiskey.

"Just fine," Jim answered tersely.

And Antonio knew right then that the banker wasn't there for fun. "Enjoy your drink. You need anything else, just yell."

Jim only nodded in response and took his tumbler of whiskey to a table near the back of the room to drink in peace. He didn't want any company, he just wanted to be left alone to think things through. His peace didn't last long, though.

Suzie and the other girls were eyeing the banker hungrily as they stood near the bar with Antonio.

"He's all mine, ladies," Suzie declared.

"Not if I get him first," Honey said defiantly.

Brenda was standing at the bar, too. "Whoever gets him upstairs is going to be one lucky lady."

The three women sashayed over to Jim's table.

"Evenin', banker man," Suzie greeted him. "We don't see you in here near often enough."

"I'm usually too busy working," he told them, wishing they'd go away.

"Every man's got to take some time off once in a while," Honey purred. She leaned forward to give him an unrestricted view of the low-cut bodice of her gown. "You want to let me help you relax and enjoy yourself, big guy?"

"Yeah, I could show you a real good time—if you're in the mood," Brenda invited suggestively.

Jim didn't want to waste their time. "Sorry, ladies. I'm not interested."

"You sure?" Honey leaned down closer and pressed up against him. She was hoping the scent of her perfume and the feel of her breasts against his shoulder would change his mind.

"I'm sure. Have a drink on me"—he said, tossing them some money—"and make sure I'm left alone the rest of the night."

They were surprised that he'd turned them down, but they appreciated his generosity.

Pocketing the cash he'd given them, they moved off.

Suzie looked at her friends. "I just wish Chet was as easy to please as the banker man."

The other ladies laughed, enjoying their easy-made money.

Jim heard Suzie's comment about Chet and quickly looked her way. "What did you just say?"

"Oh, nothing," Suzie said, hurrying away. She realized she'd made a mistake saying Chet's name out loud. He'd always told her what they did in the privacy of her room had to be kept quiet.

Jim stared after Suzie. He hadn't even finished his first drink yet, so he knew he was still sober, and he knew he'd heard what she'd said very clearly. The fact that she wouldn't repeat herself just convinced him that he'd heard her right. Obviously, Chet was one of her regulars. The knowledge disgusted him. Stacy was beautiful and loving and Chet was engaged to her. As far as Jim was concerned, Chet was the luckiest man alive, and yet he spent time here— with Suzie.

Jim downed his drink and got up to leave, his anger and frustration barely under control.

Stacy didn't sleep well that night. She tossed and turned, desperate for the peace sleep would give her, but it eluded her.

Memories of Jim's kiss tormented her.

She told herself she was being ridiculous.

She loved Chet.

She'd been thrilled when he'd proposed, and she had eagerly accepted.

But lately, Chet seemed so different. Just the conversation they'd had over dinner that night troubled her. She was seeing a side of him she'd never known. It seemed all he cared about was power and money, and being the richest rancher in the area.

And he seemed in such a hurry to get her to the altar now.

Stacy considered relenting. She thought about

giving in to him and moving up the wedding, but the memory of Jim's kiss stayed with her and would not be forgotten.

Stacy stared out the window at the slowly brightening eastern sky and thought about Jim. She had known him, it seemed, forever. He was a good man, an honest man. He was like family to her—another brother, in fact, so she'd never thought of him in a romantic way . . . until he'd taken her in his arms and kissed her that day.

The misery and loneliness that filled her drove her from bed, and the knowledge that she was going to see Chet first thing this morning didn't help her mood.

She was in dire need of a friend.

She needed someone she could confide in.

Someone who would understand what she was going through.

She thought of Roni and knew Roni was the one person she could talk to about this. Roni knew everyone involved and would be able to give her advice on how to deal with her troubled feelings.

After getting dressed, she went down to the kitchen to find Sandy already there, starting to cook breakfast.

"I checked in at the bunkhouse, and Chet was up and moving. He'll be here in a few minutes to eat breakfast with you," Sandy told her.

"Thanks, Sandy."

Chet showed up just as Sandy had said he would. Stacy managed to make it through the meal and see Chet off without revealing the truth of what she was feeling that morning. Once he'd gone, she put Zach in charge, and rode for town.

She only hoped Roni would be in her office and not out making a house call somewhere.

Chapter Seventeen

Roni took one look at Stacy and instinctively went to give her a hug when she came in the office door.

"It's so good to see you. I didn't know you'd be coming into town today," Roni said.

"Neither did I until this morning," Stacy began a bit hesitantly. She'd always considered herself to be strong, but not anymore. "I needed to see you."

Roni was suddenly worried that Stacy was sick. "Are you feeling all right? There is a fever going around—"

"No, I'm not physically sick, but—" She looked around the office, knowing anyone could walk in. "Is there someplace we can talk? Someplace private?"

Roni knew whatever Stacy had to tell her was serious if she'd ridden all the way into town to speak with her. "Sure. We'll go upstairs."

She turned her office sign to CLOSED and led the way up to the sitting room. Stacy sat on the sofa while Roni took the chair across from her. She could tell Stacy was nervous and deeply upset about something.

"What is it? What's troubling you?" Roni asked encouragingly.

Her concerned, gentle tone touched Stacy's heart. It had been so long since her mother had died and she'd had any real female companionship. She'd found it again now—with Roni.

"If I knew what it was, I'd fix it," she began painfully. "It's just everything that's happened. It was terrible enough when Walker was sent to prison, but now, to know he's. dead and all because someone framed him for a murder he didn't commit—" She gave a weary shake of her head as she looked at Roni, her expression bleak. "And now Chet—"

"What about Chet?" Roni urged her to go on, surprised to hear there was trouble between the couple.

Stacy started by making excuses for him. "I know he's being kind and trying to take care of me, but he wants to move our wedding date up. He doesn't like me being alone at the ranch. He thinks it would be better if we just eloped."

"He loves you," Roni said, trying to be helpful.

"I know, but after everything that's happened I'm just not ready to think about getting married right now. I know Chet's excited about it. He's impressed that we're going to have the biggest ranch around, but I don't care about that. I keep expecting Walker to ride up like he always did—I keep expecting him to come home."

Roni completely understood. "I feel the same

way, too. I still can't believe he's gone. I don't want to believe it."

Stacy lifted her gaze to Roni's. "I don't either."

They shared a deep, heartfelt moment of complete understanding in their loss of the man they both loved.

"And then . . ." Stacy went on, her voice emotional and a little shaky. "And then, there's Jim."

"What about Jim?" Roni was surprised that Stacy had brought him up. He had been so supportive of them during this terrible time. She couldn't imagine why Stacy was upset with him.

Stacy looked up at her, seeming torn about whether to go on.

"What is it?" Roni asked.

"He kissed me," she whispered.

"Jim kissed you?" Roni repeated, completely surprised by the revelation.

"Yes."

"How did you feel about it?" Roni asked.

"I don't know."

"What did Jim say?"

"He actually apologized and said it should never have happened!" Stacy still couldn't believe how much his words had hurt.

"He was being a gentleman," Roni suggested.

"But how could he have regretted it?"

Roni couldn't help smiling slightly. "Jim regretted doing something that might compromise your honor. You're engaged to another man. He knows that. He would never do anything to hurt you. He would never take advantage of you."

Stacy looked down at the engagement ring Chet had given her.

"Do you love Chet?" Roni asked, voicing the hardest question.

Stacy was silent for a long time before finally answering, "I'm not sure anymore. Everything is so confusing—"

"Sometimes life is hard, and there are no simple solutions," Roni told her. "You've been through a terrible time lately, and the decisions you're being forced to make now are big ones that are going to affect the rest of your life."

"That's why I needed to talk to you. I don't know what to do. When Chet first proposed, it was so romantic, but he's changed since Walker's been gone."

"Like I said, he loves you, and I think he's concerned about you."

"If he's so concerned about me, why doesn't he try to help me, instead of putting more pressure on me?"

"I would imagine, to his way of thinking, marrying you would be helping. He figures you need a man around to run things."

"My father and Walker taught me all I need to know about running the ranch. With Zach and the boys, the Dollar will be fine. I expected Chet to understand what I was going through, losing my brother this way—"

"What are you going to do?"

Stacy looked down again at the ring she wore. "I don't know."

Roni was quiet for a moment, and then advised

her, "Pray on it. Pray for the fortitude to get through this hard time and to do the right thing."

"But how do I know what the right thing is?"

Roni met her troubled gaze and answered, "Follow your heart."

Stacy sighed. Until Jim had kissed her, she'd thought she *was* following her heart.

"You're a strong woman, Stacy. Walker was so proud of you."

"I was proud of him, too. It wasn't easy for him, coming to live with us like he had to do, but he did it, and he turned out to be a fine man."

"Yes, he did. I'll never stop missing him," Roni admitted.

Stacy reached out to Roni and hugged her. "Thank you."

"For what?"

"For being my friend—and Walker's."

They talked for a little while longer, then Stacy started back to the ranch.

The ride gave her plenty of time to think about what Roni had told her. She had to follow her heart.

Three days later, Stacy was hard at work in the stable when she heard one of the men call out that Chet was coming. Stacy couldn't decide if she was glad or bothered by his unexpected visit. She'd spent these last days hard at work on the ranch, using the time to try to figure out what she wanted for her future, and she had come up with no real answer. True, the memory of Jim's kiss was still with her, but so was his quick expression of regret. If only . . . She pushed thoughts of Jim away as she went to welcome Chet.

"Afternoon, cowboy," she called out with a smile as he reined in nearby. "I didn't expect to see you again so soon."

Chet quickly dismounted and went to her. He was aware of the ranch hands working near them, so he didn't kiss her. "I've got some news."

She could sense his excitement. "Let's go up to the house."

"Good idea," he agreed.

When they'd moved inside, he grabbed her and gave her a quick kiss.

"That's just what I needed," he told her with a grin. "Now, sit down, this is important."

"All right," Stacy agreed, going to sit in the parlor and watching him a bit warily as he sat down beside her.

"I was in town today and heard that the Thompson place is about to be autioned off—and it's going cheap. We can buy it up right now and have—"

"Stop!" She couldn't believe after everything she'd said to him the last time they were together that he was still thinking about buying the other ranch.

"What?" Chet looked at her, frowning.

"Please stop this!"

"Stop what? What are you talking about?" He was surprised by her anger.

"I'm talking about the big plans you've got! Just stop it! I'm still in mourning. My brother—an innocent man—died for no good reason, and all you can think about is buying the Thompson place!"

"Stacy," he began tersely, "this is important."

"Not to me, it isn't," she told him fiercely.

"What are you going to do, crawl in a hole and stay there forever just because your brother's dead?"

His snide comment stabbed at her heart, angering her even more.

"Chet—"

"You've got to get over it—"

"Get over my brother being convicted of a crime he didn't commit and then dying while he's in prison? I never even got to tell him good-bye!"

"Stacy, we can't change anything that's happened. We can only start living again and look to the future. We're going to have a wonderful life together, and buying up the Thompson place is part of it. We've got to act quickly on this."

"*Don't you understand?* I don't want to act quickly on this!" she countered, her fury growing at his arrogance. "I don't want to act on this at all! I'm not interested in buying that ranch! I've got all I need right here on the Dollar!"

He tried a coaxing tone on her. "Stacy, you don't know what you're saying."

It didn't work.

"I know what I'm saying, Chet," she countered. "And I know I'm sick and tired of you trying to tell me what to do!"

"Somebody has to!"

She stood up and glared down at him, the look in her eyes icy. "You'd better go, Chet. Right now."

Chet had never realized Stacy was so stubborn and had such a hot temper. He'd thought she'd be an easy woman to dominate and that she'd always do just what he told her to do, like a good wife should. He knew now he'd been wrong, and it infuriated him. If she'd been his wife right then, he would have beaten some sense into her, but he controlled his anger with an effort and tested his acting ability to the limit as he stood up, too. "Stacy, honey, I—"

"Don't 'honey' me, Chet! Just leave!" She stepped away, distancing herself from him, her body rigid as she struggled with her fury. "Get out!"

Chet had come to the Dollar in a good mood. He'd been ready to sweet-talk Stacy all he had to, in order to get what he wanted. He'd never expected he'd have to deal with outright refusal. He was going to go, but he wasn't going to let Stacy have the last word. As he strode out of the parlor, he stopped once to look back at her. "I'm sorry you feel this way. I just want to make a good life for us."

With that, he turned and walked out of the house.

Stacy didn't move until she'd heard him ride away. When he'd gone, she looked around in a blind rage.

How dare Chet talk to her that way!

How dare he tell her to get over Walker's death!

Furious, she picked up a glass vase that was on the end table and threw it as hard as she could across the room, watching as it shattered against the wall.

Stacy stared down at the pieces of broken glass strewn about the floor and knew that was what her life was like—shattered beyond repair.

She looked at the engagement ring she still wore and wondered. . . .

Chet's mood was black as he rode away from the Dollar. He'd intended to go home, but he changed his mind and headed for Two Guns and the Ace High. He needed to do some serious drinking.

Chet couldn't believe what had just happened. He'd known Stacy was a spirited girl, but he'd never figured her to be so hardheaded. The thought of being married to her and having to put up with her temper for the rest of his life didn't sit well with him. Only the thought of the money that came with marrying her made the prospect tolerable.

The trip to town seemed to take forever, and he was glad when he finally reached the saloon. He wasted no time getting inside and bellying up to the bar.

"Whiskey—and leave the bottle," he ordered Antonio.

The bartender eyed him with interest as he set a glass on the bar and filled it with an ample amount of whiskey. He placed the bottle beside the glass. "What brings you to town today?"

Chet didn't answer him right away. He just picked up the glass, drained it and poured himself another. "I needed a drink."

"I can tell that. Where's your money?" Antonio waited as Chet dug out the cash to pay him for the whiskey; then he moved away. He could tell something wasn't right with the man, and he intended to leave well enough alone.

Chet continued to drink heavily. He didn't talk to anyone, but he overheard several conversations going on around him about the Thompson place. Thinking of Stacy's refusal to buy the other ranch only deepened his rage and kept him at the bottle.

It was late afternoon when the working girls made their appearance. Suzie spotted Chet at the bar right away. Antonio had sent word to her that Chet was there and drinking heavily, so she knew she was in for a big night. Chet always paid her handsomely for their time together.

"See, he is here," Brenda told her on the sly. They all knew Suzie wasn't supposed to acknowledge Chet in public since he was engaged to the Stevenson girl.

"I know."

"Enjoy your evening," Brenda teased her as they both moved off to work the room.

Suzie was deliberately playing coy with Chet. She knew better than to do anything that would draw attention to them. She paused at the bar for a moment to speak with Antonio.

"Well, Suzie, it's good to see you," Chet slurred, leaning toward her to ogle her cleavage.

She was surprised by his action since he was always so careful about keeping their encounters secret.

"It's good to see you, big guy," she returned, looking him over quickly. "What brings you to town today?"

"I wanted to see you," he declared. "Let's go up-stairs."

He grabbed her arm and his bottle of whiskey and started to move toward the staircase.

"Chet—" Suzie cautioned him in a low voice. "Don't—"

"Come on. I'm ready for a good time." He ignored her slight resistance and drew her with him.

"Are you sure you want to do this?" she asked as she went along, trying to act as if nothing unusual was happening.

"Yes."

Nothing more was said as they went upstairs.

Chet knew the way and opened the door, pushing her in ahead of him. Once he was inside, he put his bottle of whiskey on the bedside table and just stood there. Then he slowly turned and closed the door.

"Get naked, woman." It was an order.

Suzie was surprised. There had been many times in the past when he'd been in a hurry, but he'd never been like this before. He sounded harsh and unfeeling. She decided to play with him a little, to taunt him and arouse him by playing coy with him.

"No, I don't want to," she teased, moving away from him.

Suzie didn't realize her mistake until it was too late.

Chet heard only her refusal, and it was the last refusal he was going to hear that day. He was fed up with women telling him no. He lost control, and with one violent move, he went after her. He grabbed her by the shoulders and threw her on the bed. "You don't tell me 'no,' woman!"

"Chet! What are you doing?" Suzie was shocked at being so manhandled.

"I'm teaching you a lesson," he snarled.

He threw himself upon her, shoving her skirts up as he groped her. His touch was deliberately cruel and painful.

"No—Don't—You're hurting me!" Suzie realized then something was really wrong with Chet, and she tried to fight him off.

Her effort was no match for his strength, though. Pinned down as she was, there was no escape from Chet's wrath.

With brutal force, he took her, his pleasure coming from her misery and subjugation.

In Chet's mind, it was Stacy beneath him.

In Chet's mind, it was Stacy he was forcing to his will.

His satisfaction was complete as he collapsed on top of her a short time later.

Suzie was in shock from his assault. She'd known there were other men in town who were rough and mean to the girls, but Chet had never been this way before. Chet had never hurt her. She lay beneath him, unmoving, fearful of doing something that might set him off again. Her body ached from his assault, and she was certain she would be bruised from the force he'd used on her.

Chet stirred and pushed himself up a little so he could grab his bottle of whiskey off the bedside table. He took a deep drink and then set it back. Only then did he look down at Suzie to find she was staring up at him with hatred and a touch of fear in her eyes. The knowledge that he'd struck fear in her heart pleased him.

He felt good.

And powerful.

"Get off me," Suzie told him in a low voice, "or I'm going to scream for Antonio."

Chet gave a snort of defiance and quickly clamped a powerful hand over her mouth. "Listen to me, bitch. You can try to scream all you want, but nobody's going to hear you. I'm going to do exactly what I want to do, and there's no one around who's going to stop me! Do you understand?"

Terror filled her eyes as she nodded.

Satisfied, Chet took his hand away and made short order of stripping off her clothes. He had her where he wanted her, and he was enjoying the feeling of power. He was determined to prove he was in control, and he did—long into the night, beating her whenever she resisted him in any way.

Chapter Eighteen

Brenda and Honey weren't surprised when Suzie didn't come back downstairs to the saloon all evening. Chet was one of her regulars, and it wasn't unusual for him to spend a lot of time with her. It was late when they finally saw Chet leave, and they expected Suzie to come down shortly thereafter. When she didn't, Brenda went up to check on her.

Brenda had just started down the hall toward Suzie's room when Suzie appeared in the doorway, wearing only her chemise.

"Oh, my God! Suzie—What did he do to you?" Brenda rushed to her side and slipped an arm around her abused friend.

Suzie's face was bruised and her right eye was swollen shut. She barely had the strength to stand, and Brenda helped support her weight.

"He beat me," she managed weakly.

"We have to get you over to the doctor. Are you strong enough? Do you think you can make it?"

"I think so."

There wasn't much strength in her voice, but Brenda knew her friend was a fighter. "Let's get some clothes on you and we'll go."

Suzie only nodded, and a short time later, Antonio and Brenda were helping her to Roni's office. They knew it was the middle of the night, but they'd also heard talk around town about what a good doctor Roni was, so they believed she would help them.

The late-night knock at her office door woke Roni, and she hurriedly dressed and went downstairs to see who was there. She opened the door to find the badly beaten saloon girl standing outside with the bartender and one of her friends.

"Doc Reynolds, Suzie's been hurt."

"Come in, please."

Roni held the door wide as they helped the injured woman into the office. Roni directed them to take Suzie to the back room.

"I'll be all right now," Suzie told Antonio and Brenda after they'd helped her to sit on the examining table. "You can go on."

"No. We're not leaving you here alone." Antonio was firm. He was angry about what had happened and concerned about her condition. "I don't trust him not to come back and cause more trouble tonight."

"No. He won't be back," Suzie managed.

Brenda gave her a gentle hug. "You're safe now, and we'll be right here if you need us."

"Thanks."

They left her there in the doctor's capable hands and went to wait in the outer office.

Roni went with them and locked the office door to make sure no one else could come in, then she hurried back to see to her patient. The young woman had obviously been assaulted, and she didn't want to take any chances that the man who'd done it might have followed her there.

"Let me take a look at you," Roni said, closing the door for privacy.

With great care, she helped Suzie lie back on the table and then checked her over to see if she'd suffered any broken bones. Luckily, nothing was broken, but she was badly bruised. The abuse she'd suffered had been cruel. Physically, Roni knew she would make a full recovery. Emotionally, she wasn't so sure.

"You will be all right, but it's going to take a while for you to heal," she explained as she helped her patient to sit back up. "Suzie, what happened? Who did this to you?"

Suzie had been mostly quiet while Roni examined her, but at her question, she began to cry. "He's never been like this before—"

"So you know this man?"

Suzie managed to nod. "I don't know what happened tonight. He was in a strange mood. Usually, he doesn't want anyone to know he's there with me, but tonight—tonight, everything was different. He was so angry, and he just started slapping me for no reason—"

"Do you want to tell the sheriff?"

"No!" she gasped. "Oh, no, I could never do that. Antonio said he'd never let him set foot in the

Ace High again. It's just that—" Suzie paused and stared around herself.

Roni could tell she was still recovering from the shock of it all.

"I know some of the other girls have had to deal with men who get rough with them, but I never thought Chet would do anything like this. Not Chet."

"Chet Harrison?" Roni repeated, stunned and horrified by her revelation.

Suzie nodded miserably.

Roni struggled to control her reaction to the news. She couldn't let the other woman see how it upset her. Roni knew now it was no wonder Stacy had been having second thoughts about marrying Chet. Her friend must have sensed something wasn't right about him. There was obviously more to Chet than anyone had known.

Roni gave Suzie some medication for pain and told her bed rest would be the best thing for her during the next few days. She helped her down off the examining table.

Suzie steadied herself and looked up at the doctor. "Thank you for everything."

"You be careful." Roni helped her out into the outer office where Antonio and Brenda were waiting for her.

"How is she?" Brenda asked, quickly going to her friend's side.

"She's going to be all right," Roni told them.

Antonio came to help Suzie, too. He looked up at the doctor and thanked her before starting to lead Suzie from the office.

Roni unlocked the door and watched them move off down the street for a moment. Then she went back inside and stood just inside the door, staring around with unseeing eyes. She couldn't believe the brutal beating the young woman had suffered, and the knowledge that Chet was the perpetrator left her in shock.

Roni locked up and then went back upstairs to try to get some rest, but sleep wouldn't come. Thoughts of what Chet had done to Suzie stayed with her, infuriating her and filling her with a great sense of fear for Stacy. Roni was certain Stacy didn't know anything about this part of Chet's personality, and she feared that once they were married, she would find out—the hard way. She lay awake long into the night, trying to figure out what to do, and she finally decided to go to Jim and talk to him. She was certain Jim would be able to advise her.

After tossing restlessly for the remainder of the night, Roni got up early and went to see Jim at his house. She didn't want to risk anyone overhearing anything she had to say to him.

Jim was surprised by the early-morning knock at his door, and he was even more surprised to find Roni there.

"To what do I owe the honor of this visit?" he asked, smiling as he invited her in.

"I need to talk to you about something that happened last night."

He ushered her into his parlor. "What is it?"

"I had an emergency late last night. One of the

saloon girls was brought in. She'd been beaten and abused."

Jim could tell Roni had been disturbed by what she'd seen, but he didn't understand what it had to do with him. "Is she going to be all right?"

"She should recover, but I've been up all night, worrying about this and trying to decide what I should do." Roni's expression was deeply troubled.

"You've already done everything you could." He was growing even more confused.

"You don't understand. The reason I had to talk to you about this is, the man who beat her so badly—"

Somehow, suddenly, Jim had a feeling he knew what she was going to tell him.

"It was . . . It was Chet."

Jim swore violently under his breath as he got to his feet to pace the room. "That man is such a damned fool!"

"What should I do about Stacy?" Roni worried. "Should I tell her what happened?"

When Jim turned to her, his expression was fierce. "She has to be told. We can't let her marry Chet without telling her the truth about him. I mean, if he ever laid a hand on her, I'd—" He stopped himself from saying any more.

Roni stared up at him, a look of wonder dawning in her eyes. "Oh, my God. You love Stacy, don't you?"

"Don't be ridiculous," he said quickly.

"You do. You love her."

"You don't know what you're talking about," he

declared, trying desperately to deny the truth of his feelings.

"I know you kissed her."

"What?" Jim glanced at her sharply.

"Stacy told me."

He looked uncomfortable. "It was a mistake."

"Are you so sure?" she challenged.

Jim hesitated, and then answered, "No."

They were both quiet for a moment.

"Stacy needs to know about this. She needs to know what kind of man Chet really is before she marries him, and maybe she needs to know how you really feel about her."

"I'll ride out and talk to her today," he said, not at all sure how he would handle the revelations that must be made.

"Are you going to talk to her about everything?" she challenged, smiling at him sweetly.

"Roni, I don't know. I'll see when I get there."

"Do you want me to go with you?" she offered.

"No. This is going to be hard enough as it is."

Roni got up and went to him. "Thank you. And let me know how it goes when you get back."

"I will."

She left him, knowing she and Jim were doing all they could to keep Stacy safe, just as Walker had asked them to.

Stacy and Jim stood facing each other, alone in the stable of the Dollar. She wasn't overly glad to see him, considering how he'd acted the last time they'd been together, and she wasn't sure what to expect from him today.

"What is it? Why are you here?" she challenged a bit coldly.

"Roni came to see me this morning."

"So?"

"Something happened in town that she thought you ought to know about."

"What happened?" She was uneasy as she waited to hear his news.

"It's about Chet," Jim began.

"What about Chet?"

He knew it was an ugly tale, but he also knew she had to hear the truth. He quickly filled her in on what Roni had told him about the saloon girl's brutal encounter with Chet.

Stacy was glad they were alone in the stable as she listened to his horrible tale. "That can't be true," she denied.

He understood her pain at hearing the truth. "I wish it wasn't, but it is."

"Chet would never deliberately hurt anyone."

"Stacy, I know this is hard for you to accept, but Roni believed you needed to know what happened."

"Why would Chet do such a thing? It doesn't make any sense," she countered, trying to defend the man she'd agreed to marry.

"From what Roni told me, the girl said Chet was acting strangely, and when she got him upstairs, he started beating her."

Stacy cringed, completely disgusted with Chet.

Then she frowned as she remembered how angry she'd gotten with him over his plan to buy the Thompson place, and how she'd practically thrown him out of the house. He had seemed calm enough when he'd left her, but what if—

Jim saw the change in her expression, and he wondered at it. "What are you thinking?"

"Chet and I did have a big argument before he left here yesterday," she told him.

"What about?"

"He came out to see me, and he was all excited about the Thompson place going up for sale. He wanted to buy it, but I told him no. I've got enough to handle just running the Dollar. I don't need or want the Thompson ranch, too."

Jim remembered the conversation he'd had with Chet at the bank some weeks before. "Did you know he came to me a while back and wanted to take out a loan to buy the Thompson ranch?"

Stacy looked up at him in surprise. "No. Chet never said a word to me about taking out a loan."

"He tried to buy it on his own, but I was hesitant to give him a loan since he doesn't have the collateral he needs to finance it. He said he'd have the Dollar soon and believed that would be enough, but I told him since you two weren't married yet, you were going to have to sign on the loan for him in order to get the money. He didn't say much at the time, but now—"

"He what? He wanted to put my ranch up as collateral?"

"That's right."

"What do you mean he couldn't use his own ranch to back the loan?"

"He owes too much on his place."

"I can't believe any of this. I know he has big plans for our future, but I never—" She turned away from Jim, outraged by what she was learning about Chet's secret activities.

Jim could tell she was deeply troubled by his revelations. "Stacy, I'm sorry I had to be the one to tell you all this." He went to her and put a hand on her shoulder to turn her back to him.

She looked up at him.

Jim saw her strained expression. He wanted to comfort her, to find a way to make things better for her. He slowly drew her closer.

Stacy had been so hurt by his apology the last time he'd kissed her, she wasn't sure what to expect from him now. She watched him cautiously.

Jim bent to her and sought her lips in a gentle exchange.

Stacy knew she should move away from him.

She was still engaged to Chet, and it was wrong for her to feel this way about Jim.

But at that moment she didn't care.

She just needed the peace she found in the haven of Jim's embrace.

It was the distant sound of one of the ranch hands returning that finally drove them apart.

Jim's expression was serious as he gazed down at her. He knew she was deeply troubled by everything she'd learned. "If you need anything . . ."

Stacy was confused and conflicted by all that had

happened, and she could only nod to him as he turned to leave her.

Zach came into the stable a few minutes later. "Stacy, is everything all right? I just saw Jim leaving."

"Everything's fine."

She answered him so quickly, Zach didn't really believe her, but he didn't pressure her. He went on back to work.

Stacy returned to her work, too, but her thoughts stayed on the news about Chet and the unnerving reality that she must break off their engagement as soon as possible.

Chapter Nineteen

It was well after dark as Walker covered the final miles to Two Guns. He wanted to race back into town to Roni, but he knew he was a wanted man. He had no doubt the prison authorities were still searching for him, and he was sure they would be watching the Dollar and Two Guns for any sign of his return. He moved slowly and quietly, not wanting to draw any attention to himself.

It was after midnight when he reached the outskirts of town.

He left his horse tied up a few streets from Roni's office and then moved in silence through the deserted alleyways, taking care to stay in the shadows.

He took no risk.

He had come too far to get caught now.

Walker made his way to the back of Roni's office. He'd been worried that she might have a late-night patient, and he was glad to see that it was dark inside. The second-floor windows were open, so he climbed up on the small porch railing and then pulled himself onto the roof. He stayed down low as he edged toward the nearest window and slipped inside without being seen.

Walker stood unmoving just inside the window of the sitting room. He waited for any sounds of Roni moving around somewhere, but the house was quiet. Ever so cautiously he made his way down the hall to her bedroom. The door was open and he looked in, expecting to find her asleep in her bed. He was surprised and disappointed when he discovered it was unoccupied. He realized then that she was probably out making an emergency call. There was no way of telling what time she would be back.

Trail weary as he was, Walker took the time to get cleaned up as best he could, and then settled in to await her return.

Roni had known from the beginning that her calling to be a doctor would be a hard one. Growing up, she'd watched her father deal with the pain of losing a patient, and as she made her way home now through the deserted streets of town, she was saddened by the death of the elderly patient she'd been caring for. The woman who'd just passed away had known her time was near, but it was never easy to be parted from a loved one, even when the parting was not unexpected.

The thought of the family's loss stirred her memories of Walker, and the sadness that gripped her deepened. Roni wondered if she would ever get over losing him, and, even as she thought it, a part of her rebelled against the reality that he was dead. Deep

in her heart, she clung to the wild hope that the no-
tification of his death had been a mistake and that
he'd escaped and would come back to her. Logi-
cally, Roni knew it was crazy to harbor such a fan-
tasy, but she couldn't let go of the hope. She loved
Walker. She always would. He seemed to be always
there, hovering in her thoughts. There were times
when it even seemed as if she could feel his very
presence with her. Roni let herself imagine that if
she turned around she would find Walker there. Of
course she never would, but she couldn't let him
go—not yet.

Roni unlocked her office and let herself in. She
locked the door behind her and didn't bother to
light a lamp. She knew where everything was. Leaving her bag behind, she went upstairs to go to bed.
It had been a long day.

Walker heard her come in downstairs and quickly
moved into the extra bedroom at the end of the hall
to stay out of sight. He didn't want to frighten her,
but he had to make sure she was alone and that it
was safe before he revealed himself.

Roni reached the top of the stairs and went into
her bedroom. She made her way to the night table
and started to take out a match to light the lamp.

Walker moved out of the other room to stand in
her doorway.

"Roni."

The sound of his voice shocked her, and Roni
spun around to find a tall, broad-shouldered, shad-
owy figure standing in her bedroom doorway.

"Walker?"

For a moment, she remained frozen in place, unable to believe what she was seeing.

Walker is dead.

He can't be here with me.

But he was.

The moment Roni realized this was no dream, she ran straight into his waiting arms. "Oh, Walker, you're here! You're really here!"

Walker enfolded her in his arms, holding her to his heart.

Roni found herself crushed against his chest, and she clung to him, never wanting to let him go.

Walker didn't speak.

He couldn't.

He could only show her what she meant to him. He bent to her and kissed her, his mouth moving over hers in a hungry, possessive kiss that left her breathless.

When at last they parted, Roni looked up at him, her expression one of awe and wonder. Joy filled her heart and soul. "I can't believe you're real."

"I'm real," he told her, his voice husky with emotion.

Unable to resist, he kissed her again. It was deep and heartfelt, and told her without words the depth of his feelings for her.

Roni returned his kiss with abandon, wanting to get as close to him as she could. She never wanted to let him go. She wanted to stay in his arms forever.

"They told us you were dead," she managed in a tear-choked voice. She was surprised when he stiffened at her words.

"What?" Walker was shocked by the revelation.

Roni drew back to look up at him. When she spoke, the words were torn from her. "A telegram came from the prison authorities. It said that you'd drowned while you were working on the chain gang."

"So they think I'm dead." He was amazed, and a tremendous sense of relief swept through him. All this time he'd feared the prison guards were on his trail, tracking him relentlessly.

"Oh, Walker, I never wanted to believe it. I love you." She cried tears of gratitude as she realized the wonderful gift she'd been given.

Her love had come back to her.

Her prayers had been answered.

"I love you, too," he told her, gazing down at her. During all those tortured days in prison, he'd dreamt of this moment, of having Roni in his arms, of loving her. "Will you marry me, Roni?"

All the love she felt for him shone in her eyes as she answered, "Yes. Yes, oh, yes, I'll marry you."

They said nothing more.

There was no need for any more words.

They had been given a second chance, and they were going to take full advantage of the gift.

They moved to the bed and lay together on its welcoming softness. Wrapped in each other's arms, their hearts spoke for them as they came together in a fiery blaze of glory. With each kiss and caress, the flames of their desire grew, searing them with the heat of their need and driving them on in mindless passion.

Walker worked at the buttons on Roni's dress, unfastening them and helping her slip the garment off. He slid down the strap of her chemise and pressed heated kisses to her throat and the swell of her breasts.

Roni had never known such intimacy, and she shivered from the power of the emotions his touch was arousing in her. She helped him strip off his shirt, and she caressed the hard-muscled width of his chest with eager hands.

Caught up in the pure pleasure of his lovemaking, Roni soared ever higher. In her innocence, she moved restlessly against him, needing more, wanting more.

In the heat of their searing passions, they shed the rest of their clothes and came together in a moment of pure ecstasy. They were one in body and in spirit, giving one another the most perfect gift—the gift of their love.

When the fire of their desire had been sated, they fell back together on the wide softness of the bed and lay together, limbs entwined, amazed by what had just passed between them.

"I love you," Walker told her, kissing her softly.

Roni looped her arm around his neck and returned his kiss. "I still can't believe that you're here with me. Oh, Walker, that day when Jim and Stacy came to tell me you were dead—It was the most horrible day of my life."

"I'm glad the authorities think I'm dead. That means they won't be looking for me."

"But what are we going to do now?"

"First, we've got to get my horse off the street." He told her where he'd left it tied up.

"I'll go get it first thing in the morning and keep it out back in my horse shed."

"Good. We don't want to arouse any suspicions while I try to find out who really killed Ben Thompson." Walker's expression grew more serious as he thought of the challenge ahead of him.

"Ever since they took you away, Jim and I have been trying to find more clues to the identity of the killer, but there's nothing. I don't know what more we can do to try to draw him out."

"Since everyone thinks I'm dead now, maybe the killer will let his guard down and do something that will let us know he's the one."

"I hope so. I want the person who did it to face real justice. But Walker—" Roni rose up on one elbow to gaze down at him as he lay beside her. "What if we never find the killer? We can't keep you hidden forever. If word gets out someway that you're here, the authorities will come after you."

"I know. We've got to be careful while I figure out what to do."

The thought of having him torn away from her again left Roni desperate. "We've got to be more than careful. We should leave Two Guns. We can just run away, the two of us. We can change our names and go back east. No one would ever suspect anything. We could start a whole new life there."

Walker looked up at her with tenderness and lifted

one hand to caress her cheek. "There's nothing I want more than to spend the rest of my life with you."

He drew her down for a kiss. It was long and sweet and left Roni breathless.

"Then let's go away together. Now. Tonight—"

"We can't. If you just packed up and left like that, there would be questions. People would be suspicious that something had happened. And I don't want to spend the rest of my life on the run, living in fear that someone is going to track me down and take me back in. I don't want to spend the rest of my life knowing Ben's killer is still out there walking around free."

"What are we going to do?"

Walker took her in his arms and kissed her again. "We're going to find the man who murdered Ben and prove my innocence."

Roni wanted to believe with all her heart and soul that they could do it. As he drew her beneath him, she forgot everything but the pleasure of his lovemaking. She lost herself in the thrill of his embrace, cherishing this precious time they had together. With each kiss and caress, their passion grew until they could no longer deny the need to be one. Walker moved over her and claimed her for his own once more—heart and soul.

It was much later, as they lay together at peace, that they finally spoke of other things.

"How is Stacy?" he asked. He'd been worried about her, and Roni's brief hesitation before she started to answer troubled him.

"Since the news came that you were dead, things have been real hard for her, and then Chet—" Roni knew Walker had to be told.

"What about Chet?" He had expected his future brother-in-law to step up and take care of Stacy.

Roni sighed. "I don't think he's quite the man Stacy believed he was."

"What did he do?"

"A few days ago Suzie, one of the girls from the Ace High, came to me. She'd been badly beaten, and it turned out Chet was the one who did it."

"Why?" Walker was surprised by the news. He'd always thought Chet was a decent man.

"Suzie didn't know why. Evidently she'd been with him before, and he'd never been rough with her. After she left, I was worried about Stacy marrying a man with a temper like that. I contacted Jim to tell him about it."

"What did Jim do?"

"We decided Stacy needed to know the truth, so Jim rode out to talk to her. When he got back, he told me Stacy said she and Chet had had an argument on the day he'd gone to the Ace High."

Walker was troubled. "Did Stacy tell Jim what she was going to do about it? Was she going to break off her engagement to Chet?"

"No. He just said she seemed troubled when he left her."

Walker could well imagine the difficult time his sister was going through. "I hope she makes the right decision."

"I think she will. She's a smart girl."

"Like you," he told her.

Roni kissed him softly. "I'm smart enough to know I'm the luckiest woman alive right now."

"And I'm the luckiest man."

Chapter Twenty

Stacy didn't sleep well again, and she dragged herself out of bed at first light. Tired as she was, she found that keeping busy was far better for her peace of mind than sitting around the house by herself, mulling over what had happened.

Ever since Jim's revealing visit, Stacy had found herself lost in a haze of anger and confusion. She'd believed Chet was a gentle, loving man when she'd accepted his proposal all those months ago, but she had found out now that the real Chet was a far cry from the man she'd thought him to be. What he had done to the saloon girl was bad enough, but she was also troubled to learn from Jim that he had tried to borrow money to buy the Thompson ranch and couldn't do it without her signature. She'd seen a side of Chet lately that she hadn't known existed. He had seemed so greedy—almost power hungry in his quest to make the Dollar even bigger. She knew she couldn't spend the rest of her life with him.

As she washed up and got dressed, ready to face

the new day, Stacy knew she was going to have to tell him soon.

Walker awoke to find Roni asleep nestled close beside him, her head on his shoulder. He didn't move. He wanted to savor the intimacy of the moment and imagine waking up this way every morning with her for the rest of his life. The thought made him even more determined to find Ben Thompson's killer. He could have no life of his own until the murderer was behind bars.

Walker frowned as he went over everything he'd learned last night. The news about Chet troubled him. He had thought Chet was a trusted friend, especially after he had come to his rescue the night of the fight in the alley, but now he was beginning to have his doubts.

Could Chet be the one?

Ultimately, Walker knew Chet would profit by his conviction and sentencing, for once Chet married Stacy, the Dollar would be his. The possibility haunted him, and Walker knew he needed to talk to Jim today.

Roni stirred and sighed in her sleep, distracting Walker from his more serious thoughts. He looked out the window as the eastern sky brightened, and wondered what this new day would hold. He wanted to stay there alone with Roni and pretend the real world didn't exist. Just considering the idea eased his dark mood.

"You're smiling," Roni said in a sleepy voice as she opened her eyes to look up at him.

"You're right. I am. I was just thinking about staying right here with you all day."

"I like the way you think," she told him with a seductive grin.

It was some time later, when they were finally getting up to dress, that Roni saw the evidence of the injuries he'd suffered while on the chain gang—the sores on his ankles where the iron cuffs had cut at him and the marks on his back that gave testimony to the beating he'd been given. Her heart ached for him as she finished dressing and went downstairs to get the salve and bandages she needed to tend to the wounds. Walker didn't protest. He sat down on the side of the bed to let her work her magic. She cleansed the injuries from the irons and applied the salve and bandages to help them heal.

"You're lucky there's no sign of any infection," she said as she finished up. "It must have been horrible for you to be chained up."

Walker only nodded, trying not to dwell on the days of endless toil and torture he had suffered.

"I'm ready for some breakfast. What about you?" She deliberately changed the topic after she saw the dark look that had haunted his eyes for a moment.

"I haven't had a decent hot meal since I left town."

Roni set about fixing that. It wasn't long before she was setting a plate of eggs, bacon and biscuits before him on the table. She joined him there to eat her own breakfast, and she watched as he wasted no time cleaning his plate.

"I need to talk to Jim today," he told her. "The news you gave me about Chet has been bothering me, and I'm just wondering—"

"Could he be the one?" she filled in.

"I'm not sure. The way he's been acting is strange."

"I'll get word to Jim that I need to see him as soon as he can get away," Roni said.

"Good. And in the meantime—"

Roni's heartbeat quickened as her gaze met his. The thought of spending the morning alone with him thrilled her. She was about to get up and go to him when suddenly she heard loud banging and some shouts at the office door downstairs. She was so caught up in the sensual promise of the moment that she actually jumped, startled by the interruption.

Walker, too, was caught off guard by the interruption. He tensed, ready to make a run for it. "That might be the law—"

"No, you're safe," she quickly reassured him. "It's probably a patient, and, from the sound of things, it must be an emergency. Stay up here out of sight and don't move around a lot. Someone might hear your footsteps."

"Do you keep a gun anywhere?" he asked, still uneasy.

"My father's gun is in the bottom drawer of the dresser," she said as she left him to answer the door.

Walker moved quickly back into the bedroom. He closed the door partially, leaving it open just enough so he could hear what was going on downstairs. Though he was relieved to know that every-one believed he was dead, he realized he couldn't let down his guard, not even for a moment. Tense and ready for trouble, he got the gun out of the dresser and checked to make sure it was loaded.

Gun in hand, Walker went back to stand by the door. He could hear a man talking to Roni and recognized that it was Ken Miller, one of the neighboring ranchers. Miller was telling Roni how one of his ranch hands had been injured in an accident out at the ranch and that he'd brought him into town in the back of his buckboard. Satisfied that he was safe for now, Walker moved silently farther back into the bedroom to bide his time.

Roni hurried out with the rancher, and a few moments later, Miller and the other man who'd come into town with him were carrying the injured man inside. He was conscious and obviously in pain.

"Get him up on the table so I can examine him," she directed.

They did as they were told and then Roni ushered them out of the room.

"What's your name?" Roni asked the injured man, wanting to distract him as much as she could.

"Cal," he answered tersely, his jaw locked against the pain he was enduring.

"Well, Cal, what were you doing to end up like this?"

"I had a run-in with this stubborn bronc."

She nodded. "And you hit the fence rail when he threw you."

"Yep."

"It looks like your leg's broken, and a few of your ribs, too."

"So I'm going to get the Lady Doc to patch me up." He groaned as he looked up at her a little questioningly.

"That's right. Let's see if we can't get you back in good shape," she told him as she went to work.

From upstairs, Walker could hear Miller and the other man talking as they paced about the outer room, anxiously waiting for news of their friend's condition. A few times Walker heard the injured man shout out in pain, and he hoped Roni was able to help him.

It was some time later when Roni finished setting and binding her patient's broken ribs, and putting the splint on his broken leg. "That should do you. You need to stay off this leg as much as you can."

"Thanks, Doc," he said, sounding as if any doubts he'd had about her ability were gone.

She went out to tell his boss that he was ready to go.

After they'd helped Cal back into the bed of the buckboard, Miller went to speak with Roni.

"I can't thank you enough for what you've done today," the rancher said as he paid her.

"I'm just glad his injuries weren't more serious. He should be up and moving in a few weeks."

"Your father would be proud of you."

That was the best compliment he could have given her. "Thank you," she said, touched.

Roni stood there and watched them drive off before going back inside. She didn't normally keep the door locked, but with Walker there, she didn't want to take any chances. After locking the door, she hurried up the steps to find him coming out of the bedroom. Roni didn't say a word. She just smiled and went straight into his arms to kiss him.

"How's Miller's ranch hand?" he asked when they finally broke apart.

"He got thrown and broke his leg and a few ribs, but he should be all right."

"Good." Walker kissed her again and then lifted her up in his arms to carry her into the bedroom.

"I missed you, woman," he said as he laid her gently on the bed.

"Not as much as I missed you," Roni returned, linking her arms around his neck and pulling him down to her. She was still finding it hard to believe that he was actually there, and she wanted to treasure every minute. She never wanted to be separated from him again.

Even though it was broad daylight and she knew someone might come knocking on her door again, she didn't even think about stopping. They came together eagerly and were thrilled when they weren't interrupted.

"I'm glad the people in Two Guns are staying healthy today," Walker told her, giving her a kiss as they finally moved apart.

"So am I," she agreed as she got dressed. "I'd better get over to the bank and let Jim know I need to talk to him tonight."

"Hurry back."

Roni had hoped to speak to Jim personally, but

he was meeting with someone in his office, so she had to leave a message for him with Harvey, the clerk out front.

"Please make sure he gets the message," Roni insisted.

"I will, Dr. Reynolds."

Jim couldn't believe what a busy day he'd had, and he was looking forward to closing time. He was just locking the doors when Harvey sought him out to speak with him.

"I should have told you sooner, but we were so busy today I didn't get the chance," Harvey began.

"What is it?" Jim asked.

"Dr. Reynolds came by earlier this afternoon and asked me to let you know she needed to see you. She asked that you stop by her office when you get time."

"Thanks, Harvey. I'll take care of it."

The clerk left and Jim finished closing the bank down. Afterward, he headed straight over to see Roni, wondering what she wanted. He knew it had to be important or she wouldn't have sent for him. Jim hoped that she might have learned something about Thompson's murder from one of her patients, but he knew better than to let himself get too optimistic. Stacy slipped into his thoughts then, and he wondered if Roni had heard from her. The prospect quickened his pace and he reached her office in short order.

Jim knocked on the locked door and waited for her to answer. There was light coming from upstairs in her living quarters, so he knew she was there.

Roni heard the knock and hurried down to see who it was. She caught sight of Jim standing outside and quickly let him in.

"I see you got my message." She welcomed him with a smile.

Her happy mood surprised him. Lately, they'd been hearing nothing but bad news; it seemed whatever she had to tell him was good.

"Finally," he answered. "We had a busy day today."

"Well, I'm glad you're here. Come upstairs. There's something I need to show you."

"All right." He followed her up the steps and into her sitting room.

Roni stayed by the door and called out, "It's safe now."

"What are you doing?" Jim asked, wondering to whom she was talking.

And then Walker appeared in the doorway.

"What the—" Jim was utterly shocked by Walker's appearance, and then joy shot through his soul at the sight of his best friend, alive and well, standing there before him. "Oh, my God!"

He hesitated no longer, but went straight to Walker and threw his arms around him. When he stepped back, he could only stare at Walker in disbelief. "But how—?"

"It's a long story," Walker began.

"I've got the time," Jim assured him.

Chapter Twenty-one

$\mathscr{I}$ still can't believe you're here," Jim said as he sat down across from Walker at Roni's kitchen table.

"Neither can I," Walker told him.

"It's a miracle," Roni put in. "When he showed up last night, I didn't know what to think."

"Have you seen Stacy yet?" Jim asked.

"No. Other than Roni, you're the only one who knows I'm still alive," Walker said, "and we've got to keep it that way for now."

"How did you survive the flood? From what little we were able to find out, it sounded horrible."

"It was."

As Roni set about preparing dinner, Walker told Jim the story of his escape and trek back to Two Guns.

Jim listened to his harrowing tale of survival. He'd always known Walker was a strong man, and his friend had just proven it again.

"I can't tell you how glad I am to see you," Jim said, finding Walker's return from the dead amazing.

"I feel the same way. I was beginning to believe the truth would never come out, but now I've been given another chance to find it."

"I guess Roni told you we haven't had much luck turning up anything new."

"I know, but I've been doing some serious thinking. And after what Roni told me last night about Chet—"

"So you know what happened with Suzie?"

"Yes, and while I trusted him at first, because he always seemed to be there for Stacy, now I'm not so sure he wasn't putting on an act," Walker said.

"I have to tell you, when he tried to put the Dollar up as collateral for a loan to buy the Thompson place, I got a bad feeling about him."

"What?" Roni and Walker were both shocked.

"What did he try to do?" Walker demanded.

"It wasn't too long after you were gone. He tried to get a loan on his own place, but he couldn't do it, so he offered the Dollar to back it up."

"Did you give it to him?" Walker was tense as he awaited the answer.

"No. His name isn't on the deed of the Dollar, so he has no right to any of it."

"Good."

"From what I understand, he's been trying to get Stacy to move the wedding date up ever since you left, but Stacy wouldn't do it. And then there's Suzie—"

"I think we need to talk to Suzie," Walker said, his mood grim. "I want to find out exactly what was said while Chet was with her."

"But Walker," Roni interjected fearfully, "you can't let her know you're alive."

Walker met her gaze. "I've got to get to the bottom of this."

"How?" Jim asked. "You can't just go walking into the Ace High."

"Why not?" Walker joked. "That'd start some talk going around town, wouldn't it?"

He managed to get a laugh out of them, in spite of the tension that gripped them.

"Look, she can come here." Walker went on, "You can go get her for me, Jim. Just take her upstairs and then sneak her out the back and bring her over."

Jim looked very uncomfortable. "Oh, no, I'm not doing that. There's got to be another way. Besides, after the beating she took from Chet, she's probably not back working yet."

"I know how we can do it," Roni offered as she began to set food on the table before them. "I'll go over to the Ace High first thing in the morning while it's quiet, and I'll tell Antonio that I need to bring Suzie back here to the office for a checkup to make sure she's recovering."

"I'll go with you," Jim offered. "Even in the morning, there can be trouble at the saloon."

"Thanks, Jim," Walker said. He didn't want Roni to be in harm's way.

"But even if we do get her over here, I don't want you to show yourself," Roni insisted. "Jim and I can question her, and you can listen from the next room. If she asks us why we care, since you're supposed to be dead, we'll just tell her it's important to us to clear your name and bring the real killer to justice."

Thinking of the real killer, Jim said darkly, "So, Chet might really be behind this whole thing."

"I didn't want to believe it at first, but now, after hearing about Suzie and then finding out from you that Chet was trying to use the Dollar to borrow money, I've got my suspicions. I've been trying to figure out who would gain by getting rid of me, and other than Stacy, Chet is the only one—once they're married, that is. And like you said, he has been trying to convince Stacy to move up their wedding date since I've been gone."

"It's just so hard to accept," Roni said, joining them at the table. "Especially after he saved you both from Ben that night."

"There's no way of knowing what Chet's thinking, but something's not right with him." Walker was serious as he considered what might happen to Stacy if she went through with the marriage. "I'm just glad Stacy didn't agree to move up the wedding date."

"So are we," Roni put in, giving Jim a quick, knowing glance. Then she looked at Walker, all the love she felt for him shining in her eyes. "Do you know how excited Stacy's going to be when she finds out you're alive?"

Walker smiled, thinking of his feisty little sister. "About the same way I'm going to feel when I see her again." Then his mood sobered. "But first I have to get this trouble with Chet cleared up."

"We will," Jim promised.

Jim stayed on a while longer as they made their plans for the morning. If they learned anything from Suzie that might help them, they would go for the sheriff and let him know. They all knew Walker was still at risk, but they had to take chances to find out the truth.

It was much later that Walker and Roni lay in each other's arms, enjoying the serenity of the night around them. They both knew it could all end tomorrow if something went wrong while they were talking with Suzie.

"I love you, Walker," Roni sighed as she raised herself up to kiss him tenderly.

He held her close. "You know, if we lived among the Comanche, you would already be my wife."

She smiled at the thought. "In a way, I wish we were there right now. It would save us from what we have to face tomorrow."

"No, tomorrow is going to save us. There will be no peace for us until this is settled."

"You're right." She hugged him tighter. "There is one thing Jim didn't mention to you tonight, that I think you need to know—"

"What is it?"

"I was really surprised when he didn't bring it up himself, but . . . Walker, Jim is in love with Stacy."

"How did you find that out?" He, too, was surprised.

"It became obvious to me the night we met to discuss Chet's encounter with Suzie. When I confronted him about it and asked him the truth of his feelings for Stacy, he admitted he did love her."

"He certainly kept it hidden well."

"Stacy was so in love with Chet, I guess he thought there was no use saying anything to her."

"Has he told Stacy how he feels?"

"I don't think so. Since she's still engaged to Chet, I think Jim is waiting for her to make her decision about their engagement before he says anything."

"They would make a fine couple," Walker said, knowing Jim's calm manner would be good for his feisty sister.

"I wonder if she's made up her mind yet about Chet. She's had so much heartache lately. It just about destroyed her when the news came that you were dead. That was so horrible . . ."

Walker kissed her. "Tomorrow, we're going to change all that."

"Stacy is going to be thrilled to see you, but not as thrilled as I was," Roni told him in a sensuous voice.

And then she showed him just how much she loved him.

It was well past her usual bedtime, but Stacy was too tense to even think about calling it a night. She stayed up, sitting in the parlor, trying to read a dime novel, but found she couldn't concentrate. In frustration, she finally gave up and put the novel aside.

Stacy knew there was no denying she was worried about what was going to happen in the morning. She'd always considered herself a take-charge kind of person who wasn't afraid of much, but she was dreading the upcoming confrontation with Chet, especially since she knew what kind of temper he had. In the morning, she was going to send one of the ranch hands over to Chet's place to let him know she wanted to see him right away. And then, when he showed up, she was going to give back his engagement ring and call off the wedding.

Stacy had thought about making the ride over to Chet's and breaking the engagement there, but after what he'd done to Suzie, she knew it would be much safer to take care of it at home. That way Zach and the boys would be close by in case Chet tried to get rough with her. She believed she could handle him herself, but it never hurt to be prepared.

Sighing, Stacy got up from the sofa to pace around the room. She would breathe a sigh of relief after she'd faced Chet. She was heartsick over all that had happened, but she was also thankful that she'd found out what kind of man he really was before they'd gotten married.

Thoughts of Walker came to her then, and she hoped her brother would have been proud of her for making the right decision about Chet. Walker had always encouraged her to be strong, and she was going to have to be when she faced Chet.

Tomorrow was going to be a difficult day, no matter how she went about it. She only hoped that Chet would just go away without making a scene or causing any trouble.

Knowing she needed to at least try to get some

rest, Stacy made her way to her room and got ready for bed.

It was going to be a long night.

Since she had been beaten, Suzie had taken to staying in her room at the Ace High. The swelling from her injuries had gone down some, but her vivid bruises were still a harsh reminder of the horror of that night. The other girls brought food up to her and Antonio looked in on her occasionally to make sure she didn't need anything, but she'd been so terrified that she didn't want to leave the room for fear of running into Chet. She knew Antonio had pledged never to let him set foot in the Ace High again, but she was still afraid.

So when the unexpected knock came at her door rather early that morning, Suzie wasn't sure what to expect.

"Who is it?" she called out, not about to open the door until she knew who was on the other side.

"It's me, Antonio," the bartender told her.

Suzie opened the door, only to find Dr. Reynolds standing there in the hallway with the bartender. "What is it?" She looked between the two of them questioningly,

"Dr. Reynolds has come by to check on you this morning," he explained, wanting to ease her fears.

"Hello, Suzie." Roni stepped up so the girl could see her better. "I've been worrying about you and wanted you to come over to my office this morning so I can make sure you're healing properly."

Suzie was touched by her concern. "Can we go out the back way?" she asked Antonio.

"Of course," he assured her, understanding why she didn't want to pass through the saloon on her way out.

The bartender saw them safely out the back door of the building before returning to let Jim know where they were. Jim had decided to wait downstairs in the bar after Antonio had told him that Suzie had become reclusive and unwilling to see anyone. Once he'd learned they were on the way back to the office, he left the saloon to accompany them.

Suzie was a little nervous when Jim joined them, but Roni quickly explained he had come along as an escort and posed no threat. When they reached the office, Jim went on upstairs while Roni took Suzie into the examination room.

Roni was concerned about Suzie's health and did check her over to make sure her injuries were healing properly.

"You look like you're coming along," Roni said.

"I am feeling a little better."

"That's good to know. Just keep getting a lot of rest and take care of yourself," Roni advised. "Have you ever thought about giving up the kind of life you're leading now?"

Suzie looked at her, a bit puzzled. "But what would I do? How would I support myself?"

"You could leave Two Guns and start a whole new life in another town. There are other ways you could make a living. You could become a cook or a housekeeper," she suggested.

"I don't know . . ."

"Think about it. I'd be glad to help you get a new start."

"You would?"

"Yes. I would."

Suzie nodded, unsure what to do. "I will think about it. Can I go now? Are you done?"

"There is one more thing. I need you to come with me for a moment." Roni led the way from the room.

"All right." She was a bit hesitant, but she trusted the doctor, so she followed her upstairs. "Why are we going up here?"

"Jim and I want to speak with you privately," Roni explained. She took Suzie into the sitting room and had her sit on the sofa.

"Why?"

"Because we believe Walker was framed for Ben's murder and we think you can help us prove it," Jim answered.

Chapter Twenty-two

$\mathcal{B}$ut Walker's dead now. Why do you care?" Suzie demanded.

"We care because the real killer is still out there," Jim put in.

Roni added, "And we can't let him get away with this—"

"I don't understand. What does this have to do with me?" Suzie was visibly shaken.

"Suzie," Roni pleaded, "Jim and I need to know exactly what happened the night Chet assaulted you. Did he say anything unusual while he was with you? Was he angry about something, or with someone in particular?"

"You think Chet might be involved with the murder?" She looked quickly from one to the other of them.

"That's what I'm trying to find out," Roni answered.

Suzie frowned. "You know, the night Ben was killed, Chet was with me for a while. He showed up late and didn't stay too long. I remember mentioning to him that Ben's men were still there in the saloon, but that Ben had ridden home."

Jim and Roni exchanged knowing looks.

"Can you tell us what you remember him saying the last time you were together?" Jim asked.

She looked over at Jim, her expression serious and troubled. "There were a few times during his earlier visits to me when Chet did talk about how glad he was Walker were gone."

Jim nodded slightly, not the least surprised by her revelation.

"He used to talk about how, once he married Stacy, he was going to be the biggest, richest rancher in the area. He promised he would set me up in a place all my own, so he could come and go whenever he pleased. And then that last night— He'd changed so much . . ." Suzie frowned as memories of that terrible ordeal returned.

"What did he do?" Roni urged her to go on.

"He was so mean—I'd never seen him like that before," she began. "It was strange from the very start. He'd always kept his visits to me a secret. He never wanted anyone to know because of his engagement. So, whenever he was going to spend any time with me, he used the back door. On the day he beat me, though, he was sitting at the bar getting real drunk and then just decided we should go upstairs right there in front of everybody. I admit I was surprised when he did that, and I should have known then that something wasn't right." She shuddered as the horrible memories came rushing back.

Roni put a hand on her shoulder to comfort and reassure her that she was not alone.

"I'm not sure exactly what started it all—what I did to set him off. I was trying to tease him. When he told me to undress, I said 'no,' and that's when he started yelling at me and hitting me. It went on most of the night. He was saying strange things like no woman was ever going to tell him 'no' again, and once, he did say something like—'you women are all alike.'"

Jim realized Stacy must have stood up to Chet, and Chet had taken his frustration and rage out on Suzie.

Suzie frowned as she remembered something else. "Now that I think about it, he did say something like 'everything's supposed to be mine with her brother out of the way.'"

Roni glanced sharply at Jim.

"Has he been back to see you since?" Jim asked.

"No!" Suzie exclaimed. "Antonio swore he'd never let Chet set foot in the Ace High again!"

"Good." Roni grew even more serious as she asked her, "Would you be willing to talk to the sheriff?"

Suzie met his gaze straight on. "After what Chet did to me? Yeah, I'll talk to the sheriff. What do you want me to tell him?"

"Just the truth. Just what you told us," Jim advised.

"I'll do it."

"Thank you," Roni said.

"So you really think he's the one who killed Ben Thompson and then framed Walker?" Suzie asked.

"It looks that way," Jim answered.

"Chet really is no good, and here all this time I thought he was a decent sort of man," Suzie said.

"You weren't the only one who felt that way," Roni offered.

"Let's hope he gets what's coming to him," Suzie said with a grim smile.

"I'll go get the sheriff," Jim said. "I'll be back with him as soon as I can."

Jim left the room to find Walker standing in the bedroom doorway. Walker had heard every word and he nodded to Jim as Jim started downstairs.

Sheriff Protzel was at his desk when Jim came in the office door.

"Well, this is a surprise," the lawman greeted him. "What brings you in today?" Since Jim didn't look upset, he figured there weren't any problems down at the bank.

"Dr. Reynolds sent me over to get you. There's something she needs to show you down at her office."

"Has there been some trouble I don't know about?"

"I don't think it's anything too serious, but she did ask me to bring you back so she could talk to you about it."

"All right," he said, getting up from his desk. "Let's go pay our lady doctor a little visit."

Jim was glad none of the deputies were around. He'd been afraid the sheriff might be busy and would want to send one of them in his place, and Jim didn't trust anyone but the sheriff. Relieved that things were going good so far, he accompanied Sheriff Protzel back to Roni's office.

"What's she got the closed sign up for?" the sheriff asked as they reached the door.

"She felt it was important that we not be interrupted right now."

He gave Jim a puzzled look, but said nothing more as Jim knocked and Roni came downstairs to let them in.

"Thanks for coming, Sheriff Protzel."

"Jim said there was something you needed to see me about." He glanced around the office, but didn't notice anything out of the ordinary.

"Yes, please come upstairs." She didn't offer any more as she led the way.

Jim locked the door and followed them. He had noticed the lawman was armed, and he hoped the sheriff wouldn't get any wild ideas when he first set eyes on Walker.

Sheriff Protzel reached the top of the stairs and went into the sitting room to find the saloon girl there. He could see that she'd suffered some abuse.

"What happened to you?" he asked.

Suzie looked at Roni, unsure of what she was supposed to do.

Seeing her uncertainty, Roni took over. "Suzie came to see me a few days ago. Chet had gotten real drunk and had beaten her."

"Why did you wait so long to tell me? I could have had him locked up that same night."

"I didn't want to tell you about that. I'm afraid he'll come after me again," Suzie blurted out, nervous about talking to the lawman.

"Then why am I here?" the sheriff asked, confused.

"Because I needed to talk to you," Walker said, coming to stand in the doorway behind the sheriff. He believed it was safe to show himself now that the lawman was there.

Sheriff Protzel spun around at the sound of his voice and stared at him in complete shock. "Good God! Walker—"

"Walker, you're alive?" Suzie was shocked, too.

"Yes, I'm alive."

Walker stayed where he was, waiting to see what the lawman was going to do. "Hello, Sheriff."

Sheriff Protzel couldn't believe what he was seeing. "I don't understand. The authorities said that you'd drowned."

"I managed to survive the flash flood and then I made my way back here."

"Why did you come back? If they all thought you were dead—" The lawman knew Walker could have just disappeared and started his life over again where no one knew him.

Walker met his gaze straight on. "I came back because I know Ben's killer is still on the loose and I want to bring him in."

"That's why I wanted you to speak with Suzie," Roni told Sheriff Protzel.

"You know something about this?" The sheriff turned to the saloon girl.

Suzie looked uneasy, but told him all that had happened and the things Chet had said to her during their time together, ending with, "And then he said, 'Everything's supposed to be mine with her brother out of the way.'"

Sheriff Protzel's expression was grim. He looked at Walker, the man he'd always believed was innocent of the charges brought against him. "So it was Chet who set this whole thing up. It was Chet who framed you."

"It looks that way," Walker told him solemnly.

"What can we do?" Roni asked, eager to clear Walker's name.

"I can pay Chet a visit, that's what I can do," the sheriff ground out, angry that an innocent man had been convicted and sent to prison.

"I'm going with you," Walker said. "I want to see his expression when we tell him we know the truth."

"I'm going, too," Roni added.

"So am I," Jim said.

"It might not be safe," the lawman advised.

"I don't care," Roni told him. She wasn't about to abandon Walker now.

"All right. I don't want anybody to see you yet," he told Walker, "so I'll meet you around back in fifteen minutes. Be ready to ride."

"We will be," Walker assured him.

Jim went downstairs to let the sheriff out.

Walker turned to Suzie. "I can't tell you how much I appreciate your help."

"I'm just glad the truth of your innocence will finally be known."

"I'll walk you back over to the Ace High," Roni offered.

"Thanks."

Roni left with Suzie, leaving Walker alone for a moment. He went to stare out the window.

The moment he'd been waiting for had finally come.

The truth was known.

Chet had killed Ben Thompson.

Fury ate at him as he thought of the man he'd once considered a friend.

He had trusted Chet.

He had been ready to consider him family—but not anymore.

He couldn't wait to see Chet's reaction when they faced him down.

"What are you thinking?" Jim asked when he returned to find his friend standing at the window.

"I'm thinking I'm a very lucky man," he answered. "But this isn't over yet."

"It will be soon—real soon." Jim was confident as he left to get his own horse and his sidearm. He didn't carry a gun often, but he knew how to use one if he had to.

Roni returned from the saloon and found Walker waiting for her. She didn't say a word, but went into his arms. He could feel her trembling as he held her close for a long moment.

"I want to kiss you, but if I do, I'm not sure I'll be able to stop," Roni told him as she looked up at him. All the love she felt for him was shining in her dark-eyed gaze.

Walker bent to her and claimed her lips in a passionate kiss before setting her from him.

"Later," he promised.

And she smiled in anticipation.

They left the building to saddle up the horses and wait for Sheriff Protzel and Jim to return.

It was only a short time later that the lawman rode up. He dismounted and went over to Walker.

"Here," he said, handing him a holster and gun. "You might need this."

"Thanks." Walker had been carrying Roni's father's gun, and he handed it over to her as he took the gun belt from the lawman and strapped it on.

Roni decided to take her father's gun with her, just in case there was any trouble.

When Jim joined them, they all mounted up and were ready to ride.

Sheriff Protzel looked deadly serious as he told them, "When we get to Chet's place, let me handle it."

"We'll back you up," Walker told him.

He trusted the lawman and knew he would do what was necessary to make the arrest.

They were determined to see justice done as they headed out of Two Guns.

Chapter Twenty-three

Chet saw a rider approaching and recognized him as Steve, one of the hands from the Dollar. He wondered what was going on and went out to meet him.

"Mornin', Steve," Chet called out as the other man reined in.

"Mornin', Chet."

"What brings you out this way so early in the day?"

"Miss Stacy sent me over with this note for you." Steve handed Chet an envelope.

Chet frowned, puzzled, but took the letter from him.

"I gotta head on back," Steve said, wheeling his horse around.

"Thanks for bringing it over."

As Steve rode away, Chet tore open the envelope to read her message.

Chet,
  Something important has happened, and I need to see you this morning. Please ride

over as soon as you can. I'll be waiting
for you.

                           Stacy

Several of Chet's men were working nearby, and they saw how serious their boss's expression became as he was reading the note.

"You got trouble, Boss?" one of them called out to him.

"No, but I've got to ride over to the Dollar and see Stacy this morning. You just keep on working. I should be back later this afternoon."

Chet was a little worried as he went into the house to get cleaned up before going to see his fiancée. The tone of her note wasn't exactly warm and he wondered if she'd been in town and heard talk about his last visit to the Ace High. He hoped not, but if she had, he would definitely have some big explaining to do. Chet grimaced and prepared himself to do what he could to play the role she expected of him. He'd been thinking a lot about their upcoming marriage lately, and knew he would just have to wait until after they were man and wife to take charge of Stacy. She wasn't going to be an easy woman to tame, but he would do it. She would learn who the boss was in their relationship.

Half an hour later, Chet was riding toward the Dollar. He took his time, for he wasn't looking forward to it.

Walker was tense as they covered the miles to Chet's ranch. He had no doubt the upcoming confrontation was going to be dangerous, and he was glad they were all armed. They were going to have to be careful dealing with him. He glanced over at Roni as she rode alongside him. She was a brave woman, but he wanted to make sure she kept out of danger.

"When we get close, be careful and stay back," he ordered her. "There's no telling what Chet might do when we corner him."

"All right, but you be careful, too," she returned, for she suspected the minute Chet saw Walker there would be trouble.

Sheriff Protzel was leading the way as they rode in. They saw a few men working at the stable, but there was no sign of Chet.

"He may be up at the house," the lawman said, heading in that direction.

They reined in out front and dismounted. Walker and Jim went with Sheriff Protzel to knock on the front door while Roni stayed with the horses. When no one answered, they started out to the stable to ask the ranch hands where Chet was. One of the men was already coming up to talk to them. As he drew near, the hand recognized Walker and was shocked.

"But you're supposed to be dead." He gaped at him.

"Well, he's not," Sheriff Protzel answered, cutting the man off and ending any discussion about Walker's return. "We're here looking for your boss. Where's Chet? We need to talk to him."

"Why, he rode out for the Dollar a little while

ago. He got a note from Stacy telling him she wanted to see him right away, so he left."

"Any idea when he'll be back?" the lawman asked.

"Later this afternoon," The ranch hand kept looking from the sheriff to Walker. Walker was a convicted killer, and he wondered why the lawman hadn't locked him up in jail, or at least put him in handcuffs. He wondered, too, why the banker and Dr. Reynolds were riding with them.

"And how long has he been gone?"

"Not too long. Maybe half an hour or so. Why? Is there some kind of trouble going on?"

"No, I just need to talk to him. Thanks for your help." The sheriff turned away to mount up.

Walker, Jim and Roni did the same, and they rode off at a gallop, leaving the confused ranch hand staring after them, wondering what was really going on.

"We've got to get to the Dollar fast," Walker called, determined to protect his sister from Chet. He had a feeling he knew why Stacy had sent that note.

Jim stayed silent as he rode beside Walker. He, too, was worried about Stacy being alone with Chet. True, there would be ranch hands around, but there was no telling what Chet might do to her if she tried to break off their engagement.

Roni was concerned, as well. She had a feeling Stacy had sent for Chet to tell him that their relationship was over. If that was the case, it was a very good thing they were on their way there now, for they knew very well just how violent Chet could get when anyone crossed him. Roni offered up a silent prayer that Stacy would be safe.

As Chet topped a low rise, he saw the Dollar's main ranch house in the distance and knew he was as ready as he would ever be for this meeting with Stacy. His mood was cautious, but he forced himself to look happy about the visit as he continued on toward the house.

In short order, Chet was dismounting out in front of the ranch house. He went up the steps to find Stacy coming to the door.

"Hello, Chet," she said coolly.

"I got your note and came right over. Are you all right?" he asked, acting concerned as she let him in.

"I'm fine," Stacy answered, and started to turn away from him.

"That's good." Chet caught her by the shoulder and drew her to him. "I was hoping for a warmer welcome from you," he told her in a husky voice as he bent to kiss her.

Stacy held herself rather stiffly and accepted his kiss without any real response.

Chet took her actions as a rejection, and though he was seething, he played the loving fiancé. "Stacy, honey? What's wrong?"

"Come into the parlor, Chet. We need to talk." She walked ahead of him into the sitting room.

"All right."

Stacy had tried to think of the right words to say, but she knew there was no easy way to tell him she was calling off their marriage. She knew he wasn't going to be happy, but she had to do it. He had changed. He was almost a stranger to her lately. The man he was now bore little resemblance to the man she'd fallen in love with when he'd come courting all those months ago.

Stopping on the far side of the room, Stacy turned to face Chet. She found him watching her, his expression unreadable.

"Chet, I'm not quite sure how to say this, but—"

"Say what?" He took a step nearer.

"Well, I've been doing some serious thinking lately, and—"

He interrupted her before she could say what he knew was coming. "I know I've been pressuring you to get married—that's because I love you, Stacy, and with Walker gone . . . Well, I didn't want you to be alone. I was afraid something would happen to you with no one here to protect you."

"Chet, we've been through this before," she said in frustration. "I'm safe here. This is my home."

"Yes, but—"

"There's no point in arguing about this anymore. I'm still in mourning for my brother, and I don't know how long it will take me to get over losing him—if I ever do get over it."

"All the more reason for me to be here for you," he put in. "I only want to help you, Stacy. I love you."

Stacy's temper flared at his attempt to sweet-talk her. "If you love me so much, what were you doing with a saloon girl at the Ace High?"

"What are you talking about?" Chet tensed, realizing someone had told her about Suzie. He wondered who could have done it and figured it might have been Roni, if Suzie had gone to see her after he'd left her that night.

"I'm talking about how you went to the saloon and assaulted one of the girls there. You had me fooled for a long time, but not anymore." She pulled the engagement ring off her finger and held it out to him. "Here. Take it. I can't marry you, Chet. You're not the man I thought you were."

Chet looked at the ring she was offering him, and then lifted his gaze to look straight at her. He knew this was the moment that was going to truly test his self-control, but he was confident he could convince her that he'd just made one bad mistake and was sorry. He felt certain if he played the role well enough, she would forget everything she'd just said. "Stacy, I—I'm sorry. I got real drunk that night, and I didn't know what I was doing."

"Well, I know what I'm doing," she declared, unmoved by his pitiful excuse. "I'm ending this—now."

"You can't be serious. Don't you realize how much I love you and care about you?"

"Actually, no. I don't. No man who loved me would do the things you've been doing behind my back! I want you to leave, Chet. Just go. There's really nothing more to say. It's over."

"No, you're wrong, Stacy. It can't be over. You mean too much to me. Let me make it up to you. Give me a chance to redeem myself." He approached her, his manner humble.

"Chet, don't you understand? I don't love you anymore." Stacy put it as bluntly as she could.

Chet's anger was growing out of control as she continued to spurn him. "You don't really mean that."

"Yes, I do." She glared at him, beginning to think he really was stupid. "It's over, Chet."

"This isn't over. Not by a long shot." He took a step toward her. "You are my fiancée. You will marry me, and you're going to do what I tell you to do!"

"Hah!" she scorned him. "Take your ring and go. I have nothing more to say to you." She threw the ring at him.

Chet was outraged by her treatment of the expensive ring he'd gone into even greater debt to buy just to impress her. He picked it up and took a step toward her. "Listen to me, Stacy—"

"I don't intend to listen to anything else you have to say. Get out of here. We're through." She started to move away from him.

The last of his control snapped at her insult. He grabbed her by the arm in a bruising grip and yanked her around to face him. "It is *not* over between us."

"Get your hands off me!"

"We can go to a justice of the peace right now," he said, his tone threatening.

"I'm not going anywhere with you, least of all to get married! I told you, I don't love you. I've fallen in love with someone else!" She deliberately threw that in his face, wanting to get to him in any way she could.

He froze as he stared down at her. "What are you talking about?"

Stacy looked up at him, her expression confident and proud. She wasn't going to let him see the fear in her heart. "There's someone else in my life. He's the one I want to marry, not you!"

"You criticize me for being with Suzie and all the while you've been cheating on me?" he demanded.

Stacy gave a scoffing laugh at his words. "That's right."

Chet was ready to slap her when he heard what sounded like someone riding toward the house.

"Someone's coming," she said, jerking free of his hold. "Don't you think it's time you left? Or do I have to call Zach to get you off the Dollar?"

Chapter Twenty-four

Walker made his way quietly around to the back of the ranch house. He had separated from the others a few miles back, wanting to have the element of surprise on their side when they confronted Chet. He could well imagine how shocked Chet was going to be when Sheriff Protzel announced he had come to arrest him. He knew Chet might cause trouble, and he wanted to be in a position to stop it. He was going to enjoy seeing the look on Chet's face the first time Chet saw him again.

The thought made Walker smile.

It also made him smile to think about seeing Stacy again.

He reined in and dismounted, then quietly approached the house on foot and climbed in through a back window. Walker hoped Chet would surrender without a fight. He didn't want to put Roni or Stacy in any danger.

*　*　*

Roni was anxious about what was to come as they rode up and drew rein in front of the house. This was the moment she'd been waiting for ever since Walker had first been wrongfully arrested and convicted for Ben Thompson's murder.

Justice was going to be served today.

They were going to confront the real killer and bring him in.

They were going to clear Walker's name.

"Well, we're here," Sheriff Protzel said. He dismounted and tied up his horse. "Let's get this over with." He looked at Jim. "You ready?"

"Yeah, I'm ready." Jim was determined to get Stacy away from Chet, once and for all.

They headed up to the front door.

Inside the house, Stacy was glad to move away from Chet and go to the door. She was surprised to find it was Jim, Roni and Sheriff Protzel who were coming up the walk.

Chet, wondering who it was, came up to stand behind her.

Stacy tensed, uncomfortable with Chet's nearness. She was puzzled as to why the lawman was with Jim and Roni, but she wasn't going to question her good fortune at their timely arrival.

"Why, hello, Sheriff—Jim, Roni. This is a nice surprise. What brings you out here today?" she greeted them.

"Hi, Stacy," Roni said, smiling as if their visit was purely social. "Something's come up and we need to talk to you."

"Well, come on in. It's wonderful to have some company."

Roni was torn between the excitement of Stacy's upcoming reunion with Walker and the uneasiness of wondering what was going to happen when Chet saw him. She hid her runaway emotions and tried to look casual as she went inside.

"Chet's here, too, but he was just getting ready to leave," Stacy said in an artificially sweet voice.

"There's no need to rush off, Chet," Jim said.

Sheriff Protzel put in, "Yeah, it's good that you're here. I have a few things I need to talk with you about, too."

"Really?" Chet was surprised by the lawman's remarks. "I'll be glad to stick around then. I've got the time."

"Good," the sheriff said, satisfied that everything was falling into place.

"Let's go into the parlor," Stacy offered, leading the way.

They followed her.

"Please, make yourselves comfortable," she invited. "Sit down."

"I prefer to stand," the lawman began. "There are a few things I need to get straightened out."

"About what?" Stacy asked, her mood turning more serious as she realized this was no casual social call.

"Well, about Chet." Sheriff Protzel looked at the other man.

"What is it?" Chet asked, playing the innocent.

He suspected the sheriff might have come there looking for him because of the incident with Suzie. The thought of talking about it in front of Jim and Roni irked him, but there wasn't anything he could do to avoid that now. He just had to sit tight and play his cards right.

"Well, Chet, it seems there have been new developments in the Ben Thompson murder case."

"What's happened?" Stacy asked quickly, startled by his revelation.

"From what I've been able to figure out, the wrong man was sent to prison," he went on.

Stacy looked up at the sheriff, tears filling her eyes. "I told you my brother was innocent!"

"I believed you, but the case against Walker was too solid, and I couldn't find anyone else who had a motive—until now." He left his sentence hanging for a moment.

"What do you mean? You've found the real killer?" Chet asked, acting excited even as an edge of panic gripped him. He didn't think he'd said anything incriminating when he'd been with Suzie the other night, but then again, he had been drunk out of his mind.

"We have," Sheriff Protzel said. "Thanks to new information I've received."

Stacy was devastated. "But even if you do know who really did it now, it won't bring my brother back."

"Yes, it will," Walker said as he appeared in the doorway that led to the dining room.

"*Walker?*" Stacy cried out in complete and utter shock at the sight of him. She stared at him in disbelief for a moment, and then pure joy filled her heart. She ran across the room and was enfolded in his loving embrace. "You're alive! I can't believe it!"

"Neither could we when he first came to us," Jim said, smiling at the sight of Stacy's joy in being reunited with her brother.

"But how did you survive that flash flood?" Chet was shocked, but for different reasons. He acted concerned. "The telegram Jim got said you'd drowned."

"The prison guards believed I drowned, and that was fine with me. It gave me the time I needed to get back here and find the real killer," Walker said tersely as he drew back from Stacy.

Chet wasn't sure what was coming next. "Who is it? What did you find out?"

"Maybe you're the one who should be telling us what really happened that night," Walker challenged him.

"I've already told you what I remember," Chet blustered. "I stayed there at Roni's office with you and Jim for a good part of the night. Then I left for home."

"But did you?"

"Did I what?" he countered.

"Did you go home?"

"Walker, what are you saying?" Stacy was bewildered as she looked between her brother and Chet. She could tell that Walker was expecting trouble at any second, and Chet just looked confused.

"Of course I went home. Where else could I have gone?"

"To see Suzie. Then, when you were through with her, you went after Ben Thompson. It was the perfect setup for you. Frame me for the murder and then get Stacy and the Dollar all for your own," Walker charged.

"You're crazy!" Complete and total panic was filling Chet. He realized if it came to a showdown, he was completely outnumbered.

Suddenly Stacy made the connection, and she was horrified by what Chet had done. "Did you really do it, Chet?"

"No, these accusations are nothing but lies. Whoever told you this is just trying to make trouble for us as a family. They don't know what they're talking about. I didn't kill Ben Thompson!"

"According to Suzie, you said, 'Everything's supposed to be mine with her brother out of the way.' "

"Of course, she would lie to you. She's a whore! What did you pay her? She'll do anything for money!" Chet exclaimed.

"Oh, we didn't have to pay her anything," Sheriff Protzel said. "She talked willingly once she knew we'd keep her safe from you. You're under arrest for the murder of Ben Thompson, Chet."

Rage overwhelmed Chet.

Everything he'd planned and dreamed of had been destroyed, and he knew he had to make his break for it right then or he would never see the light of day again—not until he was on the scaffold waiting for the hangman's noose. He knew he had no choice but to run, but he knew he was going to need some cover. He reacted instantly, grabbing Roni in a savage grip and drawing his gun.

Roni started to fight him, to try to break free, but the press of his gun against her side stopped her cold.

"Let her go!" Walker started to go after Chet, but stopped when he saw him holding the gun against her. He knew Chet well enough to be sure he would use it.

"Don't anybody move," Chet snarled, keeping his back to the wall as he pressed his gun even harder against Roni, making her squirm. "That goes for you, too, Jim. I see you're packin' today. Expecting trouble, were you?" He looked at the banker, who was wearing his gun belt.

"Let her go," the sheriff ordered. "There's no way out of this for you, so you might as well come back to town with me peaceably."

"I'm not going anywhere with you! I'm leaving and I'm taking the doc here with me. If anybody tries to stop me, she'll be the first one to take a bullet," he threatened, looking arrogantly at Walker. "You willing to risk that?"

Chet had already proven he was a cold-blooded killer, so there was no way Walker was going to let him leave the house with Roni. Whatever was going to go down was going to happen right there. He would not let Roni out of his sight—not even for a moment.

Chet started edging toward the door. "Don't think I won't use this gun on her. I got nothing to lose," he growled. "Either way I'm going to end up dead, so I might as well take as many people with me as I can!"

"Give it up, Chet." Walker tried a calm tone on him. "Like you said, there's no way out of this for you, so why don't you just put the gun down and turn yourself in?"

"You go to hell!"

"I've already been there," Walker said coldly, trying to figure out the best way to get Roni away from Chet.

"All of you, put your guns down on the floor. Walker, Jim, Sheriff—Do it! Now! Or, so help me, I'll shoot Roni right here where she stands! Like I said, I got nothing to lose!"

Roni wanted to fight Chet and break free, but his harsh hold on her, along with the deadly press of the cold metal gun against her side, kept her still. She looked at Walker, and for a moment, their gazes met. She knew if there was some way out of this, Walker would find it.

"Do it!" Chet commended.

Stacy cast a quick glance at her brother and saw the look of fierce determination on his face. She knew Walker was going to take action. Chet had picked the wrong man to cross.

"All right, Chet," Jim said, slowly drawing his gun. He thought about getting a shot off at him, but the way Chet was holding Roni right in front of him, it would be impossible. "We'll do exactly what you say. Just don't hurt Roni." He put the gun down next to him.

"Hurry up!" Chet demanded.

"Okay," Sheriff Protzel quickly assured him as he, too, drew his gun and put it on the floor. He was frustrated. He had to do whatever he could to make sure Roni wasn't harmed, but he didn't like facing a vengeful fool like Chet unarmed.

"Let's go, Walker! *Now* or so help me, I'll kill her!" Chet looked over at him, desperate madness shining in his eyes.

Walker looked at Roni for one moment longer and then, slowly, drew his gun and bent down to lay it on the floor. He knew this was his one chance to save her.

In one smooth move, he drew the knife he'd been carrying with him in his boot and threw it at Chet.

Walker's aim was perfect.

The knife caught Chet in the shoulder of his gun arm. The unexpected agony made him ease his hold on Roni, and in that instant, she jerked herself free.

Walker needed no other opportunity.

He launched himself bodily at Chet, knocking the gun from his hand and tackling him to the floor. In a savage move, he yanked the knife out of Chet's shoulder and pressed it to his throat.

Chet froze as he stared up at the man he'd betrayed.

Chapter Twenty-five

Walker glared down at Chet as he held him pinned to the floor and saw the absolute terror in Chet's eyes. He knew Chet believed he was facing death, and he liked putting that fear in him. He was ready to finish what he'd started, but Jim and Sheriff Protzel had both gone for their guns and were now backing him up.

"Don't do it, Walker," the sheriff ordered. "Let the judge sentence him. Let's do this real legal-like."

Walker was so tense it took a few moments for what the sheriff had said to sink in. Only then did he slowly let go of Chet. Knife in hand, he got back up and stood ready, just in case Chet was fool enough to try anything else.

Sheriff Protzel got Chet to his feet and shoved him out of the house. Chet fell in the dirt at the foot of the porch steps and lay there in misery, bleeding heavily. Jim kept his gun on him while the lawman got his rope and made short order of tying him up.

Roni knew Chet was wounded and followed them outside. "Do you want me to bind his wound?" she offered.

"That's okay, Doc. I'll take care of my prisoner." Then Sheriff Protzel made a makeshift bandage from his bandana and stuffed it inside Chet's shirt to stanch the bleeding. That done, he dragged the prisoner to his feet.

"You ain't dying," the sheriff scoffed as Chet staggered before him. "Let's get you on your horse."

Chet was a defeated man as the sheriff pushed him up into the saddle.

Zach and several of the ranch hands had realized there might be trouble up at the house. They had been on their way there to see if Stacy needed help when they'd seen the sheriff push Chet out the door. They stopped to watch for a moment, then hurried on to find Stacy. They had just about reached the house when they saw Walker and Stacy step outside to join Roni on the porch.

Completely caught off guard by Walker's unexpected appearance, Zach stopped where he was to stare at him in amazement. The other men did the same.

"Hello, boys." Walker greeted them with a big smile.

"Walker!"

They wasted no time running the rest of the way up to the house to shake his hand and welcome him "back from the dead." They were all eager to hear the story of how he'd survived.

"I'll fill you all in on that later. Right now, I need a few of you boys to ride back into town with Sheriff Protzel and help him keep an eye on the man who shot Ben Thompson."

"What?" Zach and the others were startled by the revelation.

"That's right," Sheriff Protzel added. "Walker was wrongfully convicted. Chet here is the man who killed Thompson."

Zach looked up at the man who, in a few more months, would have married Stacy and become the owner of the Dollar. "Good work, Sheriff."

"Don't thank me." He nodded toward Roni and Jim. "Thank the lady doc, there. She and Jim are the ones who put it all together. I just came along for the ride."

Walker went up to Sheriff Protzel to shake his hand. "And I'm real glad you did."

The lawman looked him square in the eye. "So am I, Walker. Welcome home."

It was a powerful moment for Walker as he realized for the first time he really was a free man again.

"I'll take care of everything with the law. You just get back to running the Dollar like your pa wanted you to."

"We'll get saddled up and be ready to ride, shortly," Zach told Sheriff Protzel.

A few minutes later, Walker stood with Roni, Stacy and Jim on the porch, watching them ride away.

Chet was slumped in the saddle, knowing he was going to pay the price for what he'd done.

When they had ridden out of sight, Walker, Roni, Stacy and Jim went back into the house.

As they returned to the parlor, Stacy looked over at her brother and started to both laugh and cry at the same time. "I still can't believe you're here."

Walker opened his arms to Stacy and gave her a big brotherly hug. "Neither can I."

Roni and Jim were smiling as they watched them together, celebrating the joy of their reunion.

"You know, Walker, it sure is a good thing you know how to use a knife," Jim said, grinning.

"That's right," Roni added. His expert throw had saved her life. "That's the second time you've saved the day using one—but this time I don't think it will get you thrown out of school."

Walker looked over at the woman he loved and asked, "What do you think it will get me this time?"

Roni went to Walker as Stacy left his side. Roni's expression was serious as she looked up at him. All the love she felt for him was plain to see in her eyes. "A woman who will love you forever."

Walker didn't care that Stacy and Jim were there. He gathered Roni close and kissed her.

"Let's go," Jim said to Stacy, taking her arm to draw her from the room so Roni and Walker could have some privacy.

They went out to the kitchen and sat down at the

table. For the first time, they had a moment to think about what they'd just gone through.

"I'm sorry about the way things turned out for you with Chet," Jim offered.

She looked at him across the table. "I'm not. You saved the day for me, too."

"What are you talking about?"

"I had just broken the engagement and given Chet his ring back when you rode up. He was real angry about it, and things could have gotten ugly if you hadn't shown up when you did."

"He didn't hurt you, did he?" Jim tensed. The thought that Chet might have hit Stacy as he'd hit Suzie horrified him.

"No. You got here just in time."

"Thank God. I'm glad. I don't want you to be hurt—ever," he told her. He knew she'd just broken off with Chet, but he'd kept his feelings to himself for so long, he didn't want to waste another minute. "Stacy . . ."

His tone had changed, and she looked at him questioningly, unsure of what he was about to say.

"Stacy, I love you." He waited uncertainly for her reaction, unsure of how she was going to respond.

"Oh, Jim." Stacy got up and went around the table to stand beside him. "I love you, too."

To say he was shocked was an understatement. "You do?"

Stacy reached out to touch his cheek. "I do. It's taken me a long time to realize it, but I love you, Jim."

"I never knew."

"I didn't either—until you kissed me."

He stood up and took her in his arms.

"You want to try it again?" he asked, grinning down at her.

"Oh, yes."

Jim kissed her hungrily, telling her without words how much she meant to him.

"Well, well, well, what do we have here?" Walker asked, smiling as he and Roni came into the kitchen to find the two of them in a heated embrace.

Jim broke off the kiss, embarrassed, but Stacy wasn't about to leave his arms.

"We saw what you and Roni were doing, and we thought it looked like fun," she teased.

"It is," Roni said, thrilled that Jim and Stacy had finally found each other.

"Roni and I have some news for you—" Walker began.

"What?" Stacy looked from one to the other.

"We're getting married."

"Well, it's about time!" Stacy exclaimed, excited for them both.

"I'll say," Walker agreed.

"We'll have the wedding as soon as we can arrange it with the reverend," Roni said, slipping an arm around Walker. "I don't want to let this man out of my sight again."

"I understand," Stacy agreed. She looked up at Jim adoringly and then back at her brother. So much had happened so quickly, she almost felt as if she was living a dream. "Oh, Walker," she sighed. "I am so glad you're here."

"So am I, Stacy," he told her with heartfelt emotion as he held Roni close to his side. "So am I."

He was home.

Epilogue

Three Weeks Later

The parlor at the ranch house was crowded as Stacy, Jim, the ranch hands and Sandy watched Walker and Roni exchange their wedding vows.

"I now pronounce you man and wife," Reverend Collins said, smiling at the bride and groom. After all they'd been through, he'd understood why they'd wanted a small, private wedding, and he'd been happy to oblige. "What God has joined together, let no man put asunder. You may kiss your bride."

Walker didn't need to be told twice. He gathered Roni to him and kissed her.

When they finally moved apart, Roni gazed up at him adoringly. "I love you, Walker."

"I love you, too."

The reverend stepped forward to congratulate them both, and the ranch hands followed his lead.

Jim stayed back with Stacy, letting the hands and Sandy go forward first.

Zach made his way up to Walker and shook his hand. "Congratulations, Boss."

"Thanks."

"I've got the horse ready to go, and I'm all set to leave," Zach told him. He was heading out to return the horse Walker had borrowed during his escape from the chain gang.

"Good. Have you got the envelope I gave you, too?"

"Right here in my pocket," Zach assured him.

Walker wanted to more than repay the ranching family for what he'd taken that day, so he was sending a substantial payment with Zach to thank them.

"Tell them I'm grateful."

"I will—And you enjoy your honeymoon."

They were laughing as Zach left.

Jim smiled down at Stacy, who had stayed by his side. "I understand you're spending the night in town, so the newlyweds can be alone here at the ranch and have a honeymoon."

"That's right." She returned his smile.

"Think you're going to be lonely?"

"Not if you keep me company."

"I think I can arrange that," he promised.

Jim knew these last weeks had been hard for Stacy. Chet's trial had been a short one and the hanging that had followed had ended the nightmare their lives had become. Now, with Walker back and happily married to Roni, the long-awaited opportunity to propose to Stacy had finally come. Jim was going to ask her to marry him tonight.

As the ranch hands moved away, Jim and Stacy went up to Walker and Roni.

"You've got yourself a good man," Stacy told Roni.

"I know," Roni said as she looked proudly up her husband. "He's my hero."

Much later that night Walker and Roni were enjoying the serenity of beginning their new life together as husband and wife. Roni lay in the haven of his arms, counting her blessings. All the horrible things that had happened to them had only made her love for him stronger.

Roni raised herself up to look down at Walker. "I am so happy. There were times when I feared we would never be together again, and now—"

Walker drew her down for a tender kiss. "And now, we've got our whole future ahead of us—but most especially we've got the rest of tonight without any interruptions—"

A shiver of delight went through Roni at the seductive tone of his voice. "And I don't want to waste a minute of it."

She knew once they'd settled in to married life, there would always be the possibility of their being interrupted by a medical emergency, since she'd decided to keep her practice and travel to town a few times a week to care for her patients.

But tonight was special.

This was her wedding night.

The only call she was answering was to love Walker.

They came together in a blaze of passion as the heat of their desire ignited again. With each kiss and caress, they stoked the fire of their need to be one—in body and soul. When they collapsed together, their passion spent, they gloried in the beauty of what they shared.

They loved long into the night, celebrating the beginning of their new life together.

Walker cradled the sleeping Roni in his arms as he watched the eastern sky brighten with the dawn of the new day—his new life. Memories of his vision quest returned. He remembered the promise of love in his future, and he knew that he had found it with Roni.

Turn the page for an exciting preview of
TUMBLEWEED
by award-winning author
JANE CANDIA COLEMAN

Allie Earp always said the West was no place for sissies. And that held especially true for a woman married to one of the wild Earp brothers. She had no fear of cussing a blue streak if someone crossed her, patching up a bullet wound, or defending her home against rustlers. Every day was a new adventure—from the rough streets of Deadwood to the infamous OK Corral in Tombstone. But through it all one thing remained constant: her deep and abiding love for one of the most formidable lawmen of the West.

Chapter One

I was too young to know that nothing ever stays the same, that sooner or later the world finds you. I was four, maybe five, when the Kansas-Nebraska Act brought trouble right to our doorstep. All of a sudden there was death in the air and folks shouting words I didn't understand—Abolition, state's rights, slavery—and Mum kept the shotgun by the door when Pa was out in the field. We didn't get the shooting and hanging Kansas did, but wagons headed there went through Omaha, some even through our pasture, and always there was night riders up to no good.

"It'll come to war," Pa said one night when we was at supper. The light in the lamp flickered when he spoke, and all of a sudden he looked old.

It scared me. Like I was seeing the future, seeing change, and helpless to stop it.

Mum sighed. "Seems it's already war here. All these folks coming and ready to fight. What'll happen to us?"

"I don't know. I wish I did. But the day anybody brings slaves to Nebraska is the day I start my own fight."

"What's slaves?" I asked, although us kids weren't supposed to interrupt our parents.

Pa stared across the table at me. "It's one man ownin' another. Or a lot of others. And it's wrong."

I thought about that. "Like we own Sally?" Sally was our cow.

"You might say that. 'Cept men ain't animals, and Sally's treated better than some of the slaves I heard about."

By the time us kids crawled into bed, my five-year-old mind was running off in all directions. "I don't want nobody ownin' me," I whispered to Melissa.

She giggled. "You will one day. When you're grown."

"I won't, either." Growing up to me meant trouble.

"Anyhow"—she gave a big yawn—"folks like us ain't slaves, and we sure don't own any. Now go to sleep."

"What if there's a war? Will we get to fight, too?"

"It's men who do the fightin'. Women stay home and worry."

"I bet I could fight good as a man," I said. "Even if I am a girl."

"And if you don't hush talkin', you'll be a sorry one." She turned over, her back to me.

"You ain't my boss," I mumbled, but she didn't answer, and I lay there, hearing all the night sounds—Pa snoring on the other side of the quilt that divided the rooms, the wind in the leaves of the big cottonwood, an owl calling from the creek bottom.

One thing I knew for sure. I didn't want anybody bossing me. Not then, not ever. What I didn't understand was that, when you love somebody, there's no question of who owns who or who gives orders.

That's what I was thinking when Virge found me later that night, a long ways from camp. My feet had taken me up the big wash to where the hills turned rocky, and the trees thinned out.

"I thought you'd got lost." He put his good arm around me, and I leaned up against him.

"Lost!" I said. "All you men can think of is a woman who can't find her way in the dark. I was just rememberin' back."

He shook his head. "Seems we never stop talking about that place. We're marked. Like Cain. I wish we'd never left the farm. Or stayed in Prescott. Had a family instead of followin' some pipe dream." He sounded bone-tired.

"Spilt milk," I told him.

"I'm not cryin'."

"I know that."

The Earp men didn't waste time on tears. That was left us women, but, if we cried, we did it alone where no one could see. The faces we showed were masks, but I reckon everybody does that—hide behind a smile or a pokerface. You're safest that way.

I put my arm around Virge's waist. "Let's go on back. Let's go to bed."

His laugh began down low. I could feel it moving up into his chest. "You got somethin' in mind, Allie?"

"How'd you guess?"

The laugh spilled out, big and jolly, Virge's laugh. "Because I know you down to your toes."

And that's a comfort. Being understood and no need to play games. But being me, I had to have the last word. "That's what you think," I said.

☐ **YES!**

Sign me up for the Historical Romance Book Club and
send my FREE BOOKS! If I choose to stay in the club, I will
pay only $8.50* each month, a savings of $6.48!

NAME: _____

ADDRESS: _____

TELEPHONE: _____

EMAIL: _____

☐ I want to pay by credit card.

☐ **VISA**   ☐ **MasterCard.**   ☐ **DISCOVER**

ACCOUNT #: _____

EXPIRATION DATE: _____

SIGNATURE: _____

Mail this page along with $2.00 shipping and handling to:

Historical Romance Book Club
PO Box 6640
Wayne, PA 19087

Or fax (must include credit card information) to:

610-995-9274

You can also sign up online at **www.dorchesterpub.com**.

*Plus $2.00 for shipping. Offer open to residents of the U.S. and Canada only. Canadian
residents please call 1-800-481-9191 for pricing information.

If under 18, a parent or guardian must sign. Terms, prices and conditions subject to
change. Subscription subject to acceptance. Dorchester Publishing reserves the right to
reject any order or cancel any subscription.